A Fight in the Doctor's Office

Cary Holladay
Edited by Brian Roley

Miami University Press
Oxford, Ohio

Library of Congress Cataloging-in-Publication Data

Holladay, Cary C.
  A fight in the doctor's office : a novella / Cary Holladay.
    p. cm.
  ISBN 978-1-4243-3111-6
  1. Women, White--Fiction. 2. African American children-
-Fiction. 3. Deaf children--Fiction. 4. Virginia--Fiction. 5.
United States--History--1961-1969--Fiction. 6. Psychologi-
cal fiction. I. Title.
  PS3558.O347777F54 2008
  813'.54--dc22
                                    2008011455

Also by Cary Holladay:

The Quick-Change Artist: Stories
Mercury
The Palace of Wasted Footsteps
The People Down South

Although Glen Allen, Virginia, is a real place, and Captain Cussons was a real person, they are depicted according to the author's imagination. All characters and events in this story are entirely the inventions of the author.

For John

CONTENTS

Diseases of the Mind 1

Tulip Poplar 23

Fell Down the Steps and Turned into a Ghost 31

Fanlight 37

Tap Dancing 48

The Iguana That Was Our Friend 60

Everything Must Go 78

Eye, Ear, Nose, and Throat 85

The Bell Over the Door 117

Diseases of the Mind

GLEN ALLEN, VIRGINIA
APRIL, 1967

THE OLD WOMAN CLAPS HER HANDS CLOSE TO
the child's head, but he doesn't flinch or cry.
"Deaf. Deaf as a post," the old woman mumbles.

Her audience, three white people in a long car
idling on the road beside the house, observes this
without reaction. Then one of them, a woman in
her early twenties, leaps out of the car and strides
across the tiny yard toward the woman and the
little boy. She calls, "Hello, there!"

The old woman looks up in surprise. The young
woman pauses in front of her, leans down, and
regards the little boy. "We've just stopped for a
moment," she says by way of explanation, gesturing
toward the car. "I'm with my parents, and we're
sort of on vacation." She reaches out and touches
the boy's cheek. "How old is he? I can never tell

with kids."

"Almost two," the old woman says.

"May I pick him up?" the young woman asks.

The old woman says, "Yes, ma'am, if you want to."

The young white woman, whose name is Jenny Hall Havener, lifts the child from his blanket on the ground, while in the car, her parents exchange glances. She ignores them. She is a grown woman, and she has been jilted by her husband, and she has no intention of returning to being a child, dominated by the wishes of her mother and father.

The baby is heavier than she expected him to be, but after all, he is not really an infant. Having no experience with babies, she wonders if this one is old enough to be classified a toddler. He wears thin cotton pants and a shirt that is too big for him.

The young woman says to the child, "Aren't you cute! My name is Jenny. What's your name?"

The little boy allows her to chuck him under the chin but says nothing.

The old woman says, "My great-grandbaby. The only one. And deaf."

Jenny supports the boy in her arms, cooing to him. She checks him over: he has two perfectly normal-looking ears. She once heard of a baby who was born with only one ear. She asks, "Are you sure?"

"He deaf, all right," the old woman says. "Can't hear, don't cry, don't make no sound. I keep clapping. Keep hoping."

"Can he walk yet?"

"Mmm-hmm. He does right well. He just like to be held."

Jenny strokes the baby's cheek and hands him back to the old woman. From her pocketbook, she takes some money—because the woman is old, because the baby is deaf, because Jenny has enough money that she can obey the impulse to give. She hands the woman several folded bills. "Here. Buy him something he needs."

The lines in the old woman's face smooth out with pleasure. "Why, thank you, ma'am."

From the car, Jenny's father calls, "Ask her where the hotel is."

Jenny nods toward her father and tells the old woman, "We've driven a long way. We're looking for the big hotel here, the one called Forest Lodge. Do you know where that is? It's run by a Captain Cussons."

"Captain Cussons dead," the old woman says. "Dead fifty years. His place still here, though. Stay on this road, Mountain Road. Go another mile or two. Big white building by the railroad tracks. People live there. We just call it the old hotel."

"Oh! Well, I guess we'll find it," says Jenny. "Thanks."

The old woman sets the baby down on the ground, upon the blanket. Her wicker clothes basket rests on a giant tree stump. She lifts a wet garment from the basket and shakes it out.

"We didn't stop just for directions," Jenny says,

hesitating, speaking to the woman's back. "I saw you clapping and I wondered, well, I wondered what you were doing, and I told my father to stop here. I wanted to see the baby. He's the cutest baby I've seen in my whole life."

"Thank you," says the old woman. She pins a towel to the clothesline.

"I should have known Captain Cussons would be dead," Jenny says. "My mother's guidebook says that he fought in the Civil War, which means he'd be over a hundred years old by now. I keep telling her not to use those old guidebooks. She said this one didn't have a date in it, but it's ancient. The pages are all yellow. She's been lucky so far. We used that stupid book in the Shenandoah Valley, and the hotels and stuff were still in existence. We already knew The Homestead was there. It's popular. I'm sure you've heard of it."

The old woman blinks, and Jenny wonders if she said the wrong thing. Hasn't everybody heard of The Homestead, even if they haven't actually been there?

From the road beside the old woman's small yard, which is green and yellow with dandelions, Jenny's father honks the horn, a signal for Jenny to hurry up. Both the old woman and Jenny jump. Jenny thinks of a toy she had as a child, a jointed wooden animal on a small platform. When you pressed the bottom of the platform with your thumb, the animal collapsed, the strings that held its joints together going slack. When you let go of the platform, the animal jerked upright again. She feels like that toy.

She looks at the little boy, stretched out on his blanket. Though it's a mild day, smoke drifts from the chimney of the shack that must be their home. She wonders what the old woman and the baby ate for breakfast and who else lives with them.

"What's his name?" she asks.

"Benjamin," the old woman says.

"Benjamin. Oh. Okay," says Jenny. "Bye," she says. She goes to her parents' car and climbs into the back seat.

Jenny's father asks, "Did she know where the hotel is?"

"Yes," says Jenny. "Just keep going, Dad."

In moments, Jenny and her parents reach a huge white building with peeling paint and many small balconies, evidently Forest Lodge. Peering through half-moon glasses, Jenny's mother taps the guidebook and says, "Is this really it? A tad run-down, I'd say."

"The Captain is dead," Jenny announces. "The woman back there told me so. He's been dead for ages." Looking over her mother's shoulder at the guidebook, she says, "Mother, there's no more *Captain John Cussons, Owner and Proprietor*. People around here don't even remember the name 'Forest Lodge'."

Jenny has to crane her neck to see to the top of the hotel. Four stories have never looked so tall. Once, it must have been beautiful, but now it's a last refuge for the poor and humble, with broken windows, rusted gutters, and a rooftop full of pigeons. Her gaze sweeps up and down. Huge oaks crowd the front yard, and the ground beneath them is littered with bottles, a barbecue grill, and children's toys: a doll, a Hula-hoop. Railroad tracks run surprisingly close to the hotel. A few beat-up cars and pick-up trucks are parked at angles on thin gravel near the wide verandah.

"It's a tenement, Mother," she says. "Its glory days are past."

A barefoot man in blue jeans and an undershirt emerges from the front door onto the verandah, rubbing his eyes and smoking a cigarette. When he notices their Lincoln Continental with its Washington, DC license plate, he stares boldly at the family.

"Well, I'm hungry," says Jenny's father.

Jenny's mother consults her guidebook again. Over her mother's shoulder, Jenny sees a drawing of a pastoral scene: the hotel in better days, complete with deer, peacocks, a fountain, and guests in Victorian finery. Her mother reads out loud, "Specialties of the dining room include roast turkey, corn pudding, English trifle, and Chesapeake Bay oysters in season."

"Does he look like the kind of person you want to have lunch with?" Jenny asks, motioning with her chin toward the smoking man, wondering if he can hear her. She has been told that her voice carries, and this has made her proud of it. "Mother," she says, "I doubt anything is being cooked here other than Vienna sausages on hotplates."

Yet she opens the car door, swings her feet out, and stands up on the grass and moss, telling herself she'll just stretch and have a cigarette. She has taken cigarette breaks the whole trip, and her parents have put up with it. Jenny Hall Havener is after all a jilted newlywed. From the corner of her eye, she can tell that the man is watching her. Well, let him. She can smoke a cigarette as well as he can.

After a few minutes, her father says, "Hop in, Jenny-girl. We'll head into Richmond."

"I could go for some fried chicken," her mother says.

"I thought you wanted roast turkey," says Jenny, exhaling smoke, "and oysters. Maybe that man on the steps can whip up an English trifle."

"Oh, stop it," her mother says. "So my book is out of date. So this place has turned decrepit. It makes me sad to look at it. Let's go, Jenny."

Going to Richmond has been the plan all along. They have come from their home in Washington, by way of the Shenandoah Valley and central Virginia, heading to Richmond in search of Jenny's runaway husband, who is believed to have lived in Richmond once and has perhaps returned. Jenny and her parents don't know for certain. They're only guessing. He has to be somewhere.

This man — Spalding Havener — and Jenny were married for three months before he took to his heels, fleeing the Halls' townhouse on Capitol Hill. More than anybody else in Jenny's life, Spalding Havener exerted a thrall over her—and over her parents too—so that his turning on them, his desertion, has unmoored them all. The Halls are three moons forsaken by their planet, their sun: the Topiary, Jenny's mother nicknamed him, because he was the same shape from any angle, round and well-kept, favoring a nubby evergreen sweater. For him, Jenny's mother abandoned a superstition—that it was bad luck for a woman not to change her last initial when she married. Jenny's mother also decided to overlook the fact that *nothing was known about him*. Despite his sophisticated name, Spalding Havener seemed to have no people, at least no visible family members to enhance or disgrace him.

Emphatically, both Jenny and her mother excused everything by virtue of his profession: he was a scholar, a researcher. Probably a *genius*. Jenny met him the one time she went to the Library of Congress, for the very purpose of finding a smart husband. She was nervously listening to a librarian tell her how to look up books, learning to her dismay that you had to ask for them, that this was not a regular library where you could just browse, and she realized then that there was not a single book in the world that she really wanted to look up. She was terrified because at any second, the librarian would ask her what book she wanted, and she would not have an answer, and then she'd probably be sent out of the building, mortified. Her hands actually shook as the librarian talked. That was when the Topiary, even then wearing his green sweater, first appeared and saved her. He brushed by her, spilled a sheaf of papers, and said, "Excuse me." She knelt to help him gather the papers, and he introduced himself, and their courtship began that very evening, when she took him home with her for dinner.

Jenny did not exactly have men beating the door down to take her out. Her mother didn't say that, but Jenny knew her mother was relieved that someone wanted to marry her, that she managed to get married at the respectably young age of twenty-two.

All of her friends were married already and too busy for her. Some of them were already having babies. Jenny spent all of her time with her mother, shopping and going out to lunch. She had even been asked to teach Sunday School, which was something that only old maids or old women did. That was a bad sign, and she got her mother to call the minister and decline for her.

She had nothing whatsoever to do, other than get married herself.

"Jenny?" her mother calls from the car. "Aren't you ready to go?"

Jenny shakes her head and waves her hand, thinking how graceful her fingers look when she's holding a cigarette. Why won't her mother stop pestering her? She strolls farther away from the car, as if looking over the scenery.

After all, she has a lot on her mind.

What mattered most to Jenny was that the Topiary was more sure of himself than anybody else she had ever met. Feeling wifely and devoted, she helped him by typing his scientific papers. She and her parents referred to him as the Topiary only behind his back. If he had ever found out his nickname, she would have died.

She has no idea why he left. For the first few weeks of his absence, she agonized, wept, and slunk in bewilderment from her bed to the sofa to the window seat overlooking Fifth Street. He left a goodbye note, so she knows this was deliberate. He has not met with foul play.

The note said, "Goodbye Jenny and good luck." She had never noticed before how babyfied his handwriting was, as if he wrote with the pen in his fist. *Goodbye Jenny and good luck.* High school acquaintances had signed her yearbook with more emotion than that.

He must not love her. Their honeymoon was just a weekend at a local hotel, after all, because the Topiary said he was at a busy point in his research and didn't want to break his train of thought for too long.

Yet during their few months together, they looked at houses with the goal of buying their own home. The Topiary showed Jenny his bank statements, to prove he could make a down payment on a nice house. Her parents wanted to help, of course. Her mother had gone with them and the real estate agent, reminding Jenny to bring a measuring tape and also a nightlight, to see if the electrical sockets worked. As the real estate agent pointed out modern features and charming eccentricities, Jenny followed the Topiary's gaze through the windows and out to the back yards, picturing their future children playing there, tiny Topiaries. "It's too steep," she cried, of a back yard along Rock Creek. "They could break their necks. Our kids," she said, blushing, while her mother smiled and the Topiary didn't even seem to hear her.

What was he thinking about? She can't imagine, but his thoughts must have been different from hers.

Trying to find him after he ran off was her father's decision. Turning it into a trip was her mother's idea, a way to use the old guidebook bought at a Ladies Exchange Club rummage sale. Her parents were just as horrified as Jenny by his leaving. In his quiet, round way, he had gained their confidence, commanded their respect, so that they came to rely on him to make all their decisions: investments (blue chip stocks only, which was what they always bought anyway); whether to buy a new car (yes, the Lincoln, a white one, only don't drive out into the Virginia countryside too often because the red clay will turn it orange); whether to go out for steak or have leftover meatloaf at home (the Topiary agreed to go out only if Jenny's mother would make him a meatloaf sandwich for lunch the next day). Without actually saying so, they had planned to be led by him, the three of them, for the rest of their lives.

And if marriage wasn't exactly the romantic adventure Jenny had always imagined it to be, she felt, well, successful, in having married a man who impressed her parents so much.

For the first awful week of his disappearance, Jenny's parents blamed her, insisting that she must have offended him, driven him off. Finally, after much examination of his good-bye note, they accepted her version: she did nothing wrong. The Topiary just walked out on her, on all of them. She has heard her mother sobbing at night, has seen her father deep in miserable distraction at his desk, head in hands.

They are in disgrace, all three of them. They have told the neighbors that Jenny's husband is away on a business trip, but Jenny suspects the neighbors are catching on, reading the truth in the Halls' faces.

Jenny hears the door of the Lincoln slam and turns to see her mother striding toward her. Defiantly, Jenny inhales from her cigarette and blows smoke from the side of her mouth.

"Your father is ready to go," her mother says, "and so am I. What's the matter, Jenny? Is something really wrong?"

"Mother, please," Jenny says very slowly. "I need a few minutes to myself."

"Well, you've seen what there is to see here," her mother says. "This is practically a ghost town."

"It's kind of pretty," Jenny says, "with this old hotel, and the trees, and the railroad tracks."

"Then take a picture, and let's go."

"A picture won't be enough," Jenny says.

Her mother says, "Your heard what your father said — he's hungry."

Jenny knows that her parents hate for their meals to be delayed. Jenny is hungry too but won't admit it.

"It's time for *lunch*, Jenny!" her mother cries.

That has always been the trump card in the Hall family, but Jenny says, "It won't hurt to wait a little longer. It's not like any of us are *deprived*."

Jenny's mother exhales and goes back to the car. Jenny knows that the man on the verandah witnessed this exchange and saw her win, and she is glad. He must be impressed that she knows the word 'deprived.'

Her thoughts return to the recent dramas of her own life.

Right after the Topiary's disappearance, her mother had tried to pry it out of her, how it was between them at night. Shocked by her mother's curiosity, Jenny has stubbornly refused to answer. It's practically the only secret she has ever kept from her mother. In truth, she can't remember her nights with the Topiary very well, except the way his tongue poked out of his mouth, the mouth that reminded her of a buttonhole. What happened next was like multiplication tables — they started with something, then did something a certain number of times, and bam! Wow. It happened frequently in their three months together.

Though Jenny's parents don't know it, the Topiary claimed he saw a ghost of an early occupant of the house, the shade of an ambassador's wife, a woman known to have been shot by her husband around 1890. Jenny herself had told him the story of the murder. Late one night, shortly before he vanished, the Topiary, ashen-faced, reported to Jenny that he had passed a woman in a long yellow dress in the hallway. Jenny laughed and asked, "Did she say boo?"

After that, they never made love. Jenny reached for him, those last few nights, but he rolled away from her. Something about the ghost, or his belief that he had seen a ghost, had profoundly disrupted his peace of mind, Jenny now believes, but she can't imagine what she could have done about that.

Though her parents haven't noticed, she stopped sobbing a week ago and has even enjoyed parts of this trip. Telling her mother that Captain Cussons is dead is the most fun she has had in weeks.

And today, just now, she met somebody just as extraordinary as the Topiary. More so.

The little black baby. Benjamin.

In those few minutes since she laid eyes on him, since he blinked at her and she understood his world to be silent, she has adored him. For the first time in her life, she understands how it feels to truly love another person. And because she loves Benjamin, she wants to know everything about him. She wants to turn and run back to him, every step as fast as she can go. She has never been the kind of girl who makes a fuss over babies. As a child, she preferred fashion dolls to baby dolls. The fact that

Benjamin is a very young child is almost incidental. She simply loves him for the soul that she glimpsed in his eyes. She would love him the same way if he were her age or very old.

She returns to the Lincoln. Her father has turned off the ignition, and the car sits silent, looking huge and marooned. Jenny has something important to say.

"I can't leave yet," she says, bending down to the open window where her mother rests an elbow. "I'm going to stay here for a while."

Her mother says, "You're smoking way too much, Jenny, and you don't seem to care if your father and I starve to death."

Jenny speaks across her mother. "Dad, could you open the trunk?"

"What do you need, Sugar?" he asks.

"My suitcase. I'm staying."

Her mother says, "For heaven's sake, Jenny! We'll be in Richmond in about twenty minutes. The Jefferson Hotel is supposed to be very nice. Are you still making fun of me?"

During the next several minutes, while Jenny argues with her parents, she is aware of the man high up on the verandah, observing them. Now she feels challenged by him, certain that he is thinking loathsome, even criminal thoughts.

"What about your husband, Jenny?" her father asks.

"Damn that Topiary," says Jenny.

"But you're a married woman. You've got to

settle this with him," says her father.

"I don't feel married. Can't we just forget about him?"

Her father lifts his hands from the steering wheel in a gesture of dismay. "Don't you want to patch it up with him, Jenny-girl? Don't let pride..."

She cuts him off. "I'd like to ask him why he always wore that dumb old green sweater, and who he ever expects to read the stuff he writes. I don't even remember what that research was all about." She does remember some of it. It was about diseases of the mind, a choice of subject which she found curiously antagonistic, as if he claimed to be the sole sane expert in a world of crazies. She didn't find his papers nearly as interesting as the "Ask Andy" column in the Sunday funny papers, where you can send in a question on any scientific matter and get an answer. Reading "Ask Andy," she always wonders who, exactly, Andy is, and how he knows so much. When she was much younger, she had written out some questions about sex but was afraid to mail them, thinking her name would get into the paper.

In the car, her parents hold a muffled conference. To Jenny's surprise, her mother is crying. Her father steps out of the car, opens the trunk, hauls Jenny's suitcase out, and sets it on the gravel. His face is troubled.

He says, "Your mother's worst fear, Jenny, is that your husband might have another wife, a whole other family that he has gone back to."

"In that case, I'm off the hook," says Jenny, the word *bravado* springing to mind. How like her mother to do this to her, to catastrophize, to drive a situation further out of control. Jenny retrenches. "Nothing you can do will make me change my mind. I'm not going to Richmond. I'm staying here."

Her father gets into the driver's seat again, and another conference ensues, during which her mother blows her nose and her father consults his watch.

"Well, what are you going to do here, Jenny? What's the name of this place, Margaret?" her father asks her mother. Jenny wonders when her parents began to resemble each other: matching blond bears with a subdued, moneyed glamour. Today, they're both wearing expensive brown jackets with suede collars.

"Glen Allen, Virginia," answers Jenny's mother, tossing the guidebook onto the floor of the car.

Jenny shrugs. "What'll I do here? I don't know. I could probably get a teaching job or do something to help Negroes."

As if summoned, an old black man on a bicycle glides by on the opposite side of the narrow road, dipping his head in acknowledgment of Jenny's wave.

"So you don't care a thing about your marriage. I knew it all along," says her mother furiously. "Daniel, just leave her. She can catch a bus home, when she's good and ready."

Her father is silent for a while, and then he says, "Only if we find her a better place to stay. This doesn't feel real safe. I don't like the looks of him up there." He motions with his head toward the man on the hotel porch, who is still eyeing them with the lazy attention that Jenny associates with attack dogs. As she inhales from another cigarette, she considers what the man's life might be like and longs to tell him about her own. In a sudden daydream, she imagines that he would fight the Topiary for her and win, and leave the Topiary in a green heap on the ground, like a kicked-over Christmas tree.

"You know something? I don't think there's a whole lot to choose from around here, in terms of places to stay. This place might be the Glen Allen Ritz," her mother says.

Her father asks, "Jenny, what do you say? Can we look to find you something better?"

Jenny concedes that much. They can't force her back into the Lincoln. With her father driving very slowly, and her mother fuming, she keeps pace alongside the car, her suitcase already heavy on her arm, but she won't put it back in the car. She hasn't taken but a few steps when she hears the high, urgent song of a train, still far away. The crossing gates swing down, barring the road, and her father stops the car.

"That train," her father says, as if he is really talking about something else, as if the train is for him what the baby, Benjamin, is for her. He considers himself something of an authority on trains. "Listen. That train's carrying such a heavy load."

Setting her suitcase down on the road, Jenny sets down everything—her life with her parents, her stifling education at a girls' school and then two bewildering years in college, and her married life. The only memory she cares to keep is an image from yesterday morning, when her family sped along a winding road in the Shenandoah Mountains during a brief snowfall. The mountains felt high and foreign. Such a beautiful, shivery snow it was, surprising, end-of-April snow, falling on sheep and goats and greening grass, then melting right away. Cozy in the back seat of the Lincoln, she imagined herself inside a paperweight filled with water and swirling flakes. By the time they reached The Homestead at Hot Springs, the sun was shining, and they lunched on a glassed-in patio with vases of daffodils on every table, enjoying Smithfield ham, fresh asparagus, and scalloped potatoes.

Later, Jenny and her mother swam in the indoor pool, treated themselves to massages, and had their hair and nails done while Jenny's father played a round of golf. While the hairdresser rolled a hot iron into Jenny's bangs, Jenny wondered how it would be to slip into that life, to become that beautician with bags beneath sore, ice-blue eyes, a beaten expression, her hands with swollen joints accustomed to pampering rich women's heads. The idea of the beautician's life was scary, but it was scary too to keep on as she was, as Jenny Hall Havener, a rejected wife, getting her hair teased into a bouffant while in the next cameo-pink chair, her mother skimmed through *Town & Country* and reminded the manicurist that she wanted ridge filler and a base coat on her nails, and that the two were not the same. Later, in the gift shop, Jenny's mother bought atomizers for herself and for Jenny, crystal globes that came with tiny vials of French perfume.

Jenny touches her hair, which still holds the stiff waves from the curling iron. Thank goodness she saved the wrapped, lavender-scented soaps from the hotel: something for Benjamin. She'll tell him about snow falling on the spry goats in a mountain valley, and about a woman who married a man who ran away, and how the woman by accident found the most wonderful baby in the world.

Over the sound of the approaching train, Jenny's father says, "I have something to say to you. Both of you. Lean down and listen, Jenny."

Jenny stoops down to her father's open window, her eyes meeting her mother's glare. Her father has to yell to be heard. To Jenny's mother, he says, "Margaret, do you remember when you bought Jenny an iguana?"

Jenny's mother stares at him. "I hadn't thought about that thing in a long time," she says, yelling too. "It smelled bad, and it got out of the cage a lot."

"Of course I remember my iguana," says Jenny. "Iggy!"

Jenny's father speaks rapidly, at the top of his

lungs. "Yes: Iggy. Ever since then, I've never felt quite the same about either one of you. Couldn't you at least have come up with a better name? Everybody names their iguana Iggy."

The train crashes toward them, bearing down, tearing up the world with its noise, its thunder shaking the very ground where Jenny stands. Hellbent, Jenny thinks, that's me. She straightens up and steps away from the car. In the furor of sound, she hears her parents screaming at each other.

She has never before been so close to a train, has never comprehended how loud and terrifying they are and messy too, with soot and cinders and ashes flying out and stinging her skin like insects. Breathing in the tarry smell of train and tracks, she is happier than she has ever been in her life.

As the train recedes, Jenny's father reaches out the car window and gestures to Jenny. She leans down again. He says, "It wasn't even an iguana. It was a gecko. I've seen pictures since then, and it was a gecko. If you're going to buy a reptile, you should at least know what kind you've got."

"Oh, Dad," says Jenny. "A gecko? I've never heard of those."

"You were supposed to mist him. Spray him. And you didn't," Jenny's father says to Jenny and her mother, in the hollow silence of the car, the train gone. "You would not believe how much I've thought about this."

"He had plenty of water," Jenny says. "I took

good care of him."

"But you were supposed to spray him, too, every so often," her father insists. "I know that now. I learned it from reading an article. We never misted him. He dried out, and he died."

Jenny stares across her father, meeting her mother's eyes. She sees for the first time the resemblance that people talk about, her resemblance to her mother, all eyebrows and open mouth.

Tulip Poplar

J ENNY HAS WAITED TWO WHOLE DAYS TO GO SEE
Benjamin, long days of putting her new home
to rights. How like her father to buy her a place to
stay rather than simply rent one. And never mind
that it was last used as commercial property, a piano
and organ store which has been out of business for
years. BUY SELL TRADE says a sign in the dusty
front window.

"Lock, stock, and barrel," said the real estate
agent who handled the purchase. The building has
changed hands with its entire inventory intact, and
Jenny now owns pianos, organs, benches, tables
and chairs, even a few wooden carousel horses
and coffins, stacked and shoved any which-way
throughout the first and second floors. "Old-time
furniture store," the realtor said, beaming, slapping
the faded haunch of a painted pony.

The store sits on a corner lot, where the Old
Washington Highway turns off from Mountain
Road. Her father had located the place within one

minute of crossing the railroad tracks, just as Jenny was getting exhausted from lugging her suitcase. Her father pointed triumphantly to the For Sale sign.

Jenny was thrilled. She could always count on her father. He understood that for her purposes, her new mission, whatever it was, a mere room for rent would not do. They'd eaten lunch in Richmond, then called the real estate agency, returned to Glen Allen and completed the purchase, all within a few hours.

Her mother said, "Won't you be scared here?" They pushed through the heavy, dirty items of furniture, sneezing. Outside, in the street, the real estate agent trundled off in his station wagon with signed papers and a check from Jenny's father.

"No," said Jenny. She was scared, but she couldn't wait for her parents to leave. Through her fear, happiness about her new home rose up in her heart. To live alone! This would be more exciting than being married.

Her mother turned practical. "She doesn't have a car, Daniel," she said. "How will she get around?"

"She can have this car. She'll drive us into Richmond, and from there, we'll take the train back to DC and buy another car," said Jenny's father. "Jenny, you can use the Lincoln as long as you need it."

"I'll get a blue car this time," her mother said. "A white one was a bad idea."

And that was that.

In two days, Jenny has furnished her new place, shopping in Richmond and filling the car with sheets, towels, cooking supplies, and groceries. She buys a mattress and has it delivered and set up in a huge mahogany bedstead. She creates a living space in BUY SELL TRADE among the pianos and organs. The second story was evidently an apartment at some point, for it includes a tiny kitchen and a bathroom with a skylight. Jenny enjoys sitting on the toilet and staring up at the vaulted shape of the ceiling, with sky visible far above her.

There is little traffic in this town. None, really, except for a few lumbering yellow school buses in the morning and afternoon. You can't even call this a town. It's a little crossroads of some sort, with the railroad tracks and one main road. The real estate agent told her family that Glen Allen was founded by Captain Cussons of old hotel fame, and that the community used to be known for its dairy farms. Jenny has seen a few chickens in people's yards, but no cows, so the dairy days must be over.

At night, she lies awake listening for a car or truck to pass by, but in the darkness, there is only the sound of her breathing and a rustle, a scurry, that must mean mice. She feels very brave. This must be how pioneers felt, on the frontier, in their cabins, with the wilderness so close by. They were after something big, an entirely better life, just as she is, the only difference being that they wanted farmland or gold mines, whereas she just wants to be with a little boy, a toddler that she has seen one time: Benjamin. The change of direction that her life has taken is all because of him. Her heart is a compass, leading her to him.

On the third morning, she goes at last to Benjamin's house. She parks the car in the short, rutted driveway beside the gray shack. There is no sign of him or his great-grandmother, but there is an old colored man out in the yard, conferring with a white child, a girl about eight or nine years old who holds a pair of eyeglasses out from her face as if trying on styles at an oculist's shop. Jenny recognizes the old man. Isn't he the same Negro who went by on a bike when she was with her parents? He must be the old woman's husband and thus Benjamin's great-grandfather. She will make him like her.

"Hello," calls Jenny, approaching the man and the child. They're standing beside the huge stump where the old woman set her clothes basket on the day Jenny first saw Benjamin.

The old man dips his head toward her and murmurs a polite greeting. The white girl says, "Hi," and then turns back to the old man, saying, "I do want them." The girl flexes the pair of eyeglasses in her hands, and Jenny surmises that the glasses have been a subject of discussion between these two. "Thanks," the child says to the old man.

"Lemme tighten the earpieces," says the old man, but the child shakes her head and places the old-fashioned spectacles on her face, adjusting the bridge over her nose. They're a tiny gold-rimmed pair that a colonial shopkeeper might have worn.

The child swings toward Jenny, her hazel eyes fiercely bright behind the lenses. With her brown clothes and small, tense shoulders, she resembles a cat. Jenny imagines her scouting out the mice at BUY SELL TRADE, hunting them among piano legs and wooden horses.

"I can see a whole lot better," the child tells the old man, examining Jenny's face. "I can see her eyelashes. I haven't seen anybody's eyelashes for a long time."

Finding the remark somehow personal, as if the child had pointed at her, Jenny can't help frowning at the girl.

The old man says to the child, "I saw you squinting, and I knew you couldn't see. That's dangerous."

Jenny feels impatient. To the old man, she says, "I'm Jenny. Jenny Hall Havener. I met your wife and Benjamin the other day." She pauses and asks, "Is he here?"

"Yes, ma'am, Benjamin's home," the man says, as if accustomed to receiving the baby's guests. "First, though, you ladies look at this stump and tell me how old this tree was."

All three of them take places around the massive stump. Kneeling down, the child traces the rings on the stump with her fingers. Jenny thinks of a Ouija board—you move your hand over it, you guide that little gadget over letters of the alphabet and spell out your fortune. But you have to cheat in order for it to spell out anything. At least, Jenny always has to cheat. Doesn't everybody? She feels that this serious-faced little girl would think badly of her for cheating at a Ouija board. She can't concentrate to count the rings on the stump.

"A hundred," says the child. "It was a hundred years old. Why did you cut it down?"

"Lightning struck it," the old man says, "and set it afire. Nothing to do but chop it up for firewood. Been feeding our stove for a long time now."

Jenny has never known anybody who actually cooks on a woodstove.

"What kind of tree was it?" she asks brusquely, wondering if the old man is toying with her, if he senses her need to see Benjamin and is testing her composure. "An oak?" She can't identify many trees, let alone a stump, and until now, she has never cared.

"Not an oak," says the old man.

The child rubs the bark on the side of the stump and says, "A tulip poplar."

"Tulip poplar. That's right," says the old man and nods.

The child goes on, "Real big, even for one that old. You can tell right through here," and she touches several of the rings, "that it had a few bad years when it had a hard time getting enough water, even with deep roots, and didn't grow very much."

"Yes," says the old man. "Yes, indeed."

"When it caught on fire, from the lightning, was it scary?" asks the child.

"Yes, it was," the old man says. "Brought to mind

the burning bush."

They stand silently, as if something important has been settled. The only sounds are breeze and birdcalls. Jenny recalls the old woman telling her how quiet Benjamin is and wonders how it is that a deaf child doesn't even cry.

She can't wait another minute. "I need to see him. Benjamin," she says.

"Well, all right. Come on," says the old man.

"Bye," says the child to the man, picking up a book and a paper sack from the grass. "Thank you."

The old man lifts his hand, and the child marches off, presumably heading to school. Jenny follows the old man up two flimsy steps and into the house, into the kitchen, into the sweet smell of burning wood. There beside the stove stand the old woman and Benjamin, both drinking coffee, the woman from a bowl and Benjamin from a cup he holds in both hands. Through her tumult, Jenny sees that his cup is flowered porcelain, faded and chipped, the handle gone, yet the china so thin and fine that if you flick your fingernail against the edge, it would ring like a bell. How did a cup like that come into such a lowly house? But it's in the right hands, Benjamin's precious hands.

Jenny rushes to Benjamin and kneels down so her face is level with his. From her pocket, she brings out the little soaps, and a toy duck she bought at a grocery store. She holds these things out to him but can't speak. Benjamin's eyes offer the understanding she has looked for all her life. The old woman takes Benjamin's empty cup. Benjamin reaches out to pat the gifts in Jenny's hands, but he doesn't take them. As Jenny's eyes flood and tears spill over, Benjamin moves his gaze over her face the way the little girl's hand explored the rings on the stump.

"He do people that way," the old woman says, and Jenny bursts into sobs, hugging Benjamin to her heart.

Fell Down the Steps and
Turned into a Ghost

THE OLD WOMAN'S NAME IS HATTIE. HATTIE Johnson. The old man is indeed her husband, Woodrow. Sitting at their kitchen table, Jenny learns that he is a tinker, with some self-taught skills also in plumbing and electricity, and that he has just recovered from pleurisy, the worst case he's ever had. While he recuperated, he could not work for a whole month, could not ride the bike that takes him from house to house to do the odd jobs that provide most of the family's income. Hattie reveals that she works, too, cleaning churches a few days a week.

"Who takes care of Benjamin while you're doing that?" Jenny asks.

"He does," says Hattie, indicating Woodrow, "or I take him with me."

"I'll be glad to babysit for him," Jenny offers, but

the old people don't answer that.

Seated at their kitchen table, her skin warm as sunburn from the heat of the stove, her tears drying to salty, burning spots on her cheeks, and holding Benjamin on her lap, Jenny realizes that if she wants Benjamin, she must admit these old people into her life. It shouldn't be too hard. She understands them — poor colored people, elderly, with nothing in their lives except this extraordinary child. She will buy them a television set.

No, that would not impress them. They might have a whole roomful of TV sets given to them by other people eager for Benjamin, people who have fallen short, people found undeserving of his company. She kisses the top of his head and rocks him on her knees, getting him used to her.

She does not feel sophisticated here. Why is that? Her Fifth Street address, her shopping trips to fine stores and visits to museums don't mean a thing. Here in this tumbledy cabin, it is she who is unsure about how to behave. She sips Hattie's bitter coffee, desperate to pee. There's probably no bathroom here, just a privy — she tries to remember if she saw one outside — or worse yet, a chamber pot in some corner. She'll wait.

Hattie Johnson rummages in a dark, sloping pantry and produces an ancient box of sugar cubes, Domino Dots. Jenny hears her own voice, effusive, thanking her. Jenny is careful to take only one cube, shifting her knees to hold Benjamin while she fishes the sugar out of the worn box. No milk is offered.

Coffee. She will buy them pounds of the finest coffee, and fresh cream, and enough sugar so that they can use it lavishly. She'll put all these things into a straw basket with a red and white checked cloth, maybe add a new electric coffee pot and a box of bakery cookies. And Benjamin must have milk. She has seen a milkman's delivery truck on Mountain Road. She will speak to the milkman and arrange an account so that Benjamin will have fresh milk every day, and all the eggs, cream, and butter the family can use, cheese too if the milkman supplies that. Yes, and cottage cheese, ice cream, everything a dairy produces. She'll pay for all of it and not even let the Johnsons know, although surely they will guess who their benefactress is and be grateful to her. Benjamin will be content. He will not be skinny and nervous, like that annoying little girl who showed off about the rings on the tree stump.

To the old man, Jenny says, "Tell me something, Mr. Johnson. Who was that little girl who was here?"

"One of the Lloyd girls," he says. "She real smart."

Jenny can't exactly say, *Well, I hope I don't find her here again.* It was maddening the way the Lloyd girl won the game of the tree rings. Jenny doesn't believe the child is all that smart. The tree probably wasn't a tulip poplar at all. The old man was humoring her. If she'd said California redwood, he'd have agreed with her.

Nonchalantly, Jenny raises her left hand so the Johnsons will see her wedding band. A wedding ring allows many assumptions. She takes comfort in the gold ring and the authority, the credibility it gives her. *I might never see him again*, she thinks of the Topiary, and she is thrilled. Like the spectral woman who frightened him in the Washington townhouse, he has become a ghost himself. Once, when Jenny was very young, she wrote a story about a girl who fell down the stairs and changed into a ghost. She believes it could happen. It is 1967, and she could fall down and turn into a ghost. That was her whole story, wasn't it, that the girl fell down the steps and turned into a ghost. *The End.* The teacher had been unaccountably angry with her, as if the story were somehow rude.

Benjamin will understand this. She will tell him all about herself, from her earliest days, and they will live each other's lives. Heavy and warm on her lap, he's perfectly behaved. She strokes his cheek, admiring the rich peanut butter color of his skin. She sets down her coffee cup, lays a palm over his chest through his thin shirt, and finds his heartbeat with her hand. Steady. Strong. How do people learn about babies? If he got sick, ran a fever, would she be able to tell? She's still not convinced he is deaf. Nobody would be this still, this composed, unless listening to the conversation. She'll help him hear. She'll whisper to him and hold him up to the breeze until he hears her voice and the wind. She cannot fathom, can't analyze or explain her feelings for this child. She only knows that she adores him.

She cuts to the chase. "Who are Benjamin's parents?"

The old people glance at each other, and in a flash, Jenny perceives a fly-by-night father, a teenage mother laughing in a juke joint, in a low-cut red dress and gold earrings, a young woman ashamed of the wood stove and the decent countrified old people, hungry for high times and fortune. Jenny's own father has a countrified streak. He's from Mississippi, though that was so long ago her mother likes to pretend he grew up on DC's civilized avenues. He would know how to talk with these people.

"Benjamin's mama—my granddaughter, Lois," Hattie says at last, and Jenny's vision is confirmed: Lois in her red dress raises a glass of whiskey and swings her hips, and every man on the dance floor wants her. The lights of the juke joint spit fireworks when Lois smiles.

"Where is she?" asks Jenny. "Does she live somewhere else?"

"She dead," Hattie says.

"Oh!" Somehow, this news is not unwelcome. It means there is one less obstacle to getting Benjamin. "I'm sorry to hear that. And Benjamin's father? What about him?" Jenny asks, thinking they may resent her, she who has monopolized their morning and cried over a child she has no right to. Clutching Benjamin to her chest, she is not reassured by the neutrality of their expressions. They're holding back. She presses on. "Who is his father?"

"A white man," says Woodrow Johnson in a voice like winter wind. "Lives at the old hotel. The one always smoking on the steps."

Jenny's jaw drops. Trap–like, a circle clamps shut.

Fanlight

"**I** KNEW YOU WOULD COME," THE MAN SAYS TO Jenny as she climbs the steps of the old hotel. He holds his cigarette away from his lips while he speaks. "I know who you are. But you'll have to wait. There's a party going on, and I have to help."

"I can see that," Jenny says, out of breath from walking the distance from BUY SELL TRADE to the old hotel. Yet in Washington, DC, she used to walk much farther than this. She sinks down on the steps of the verandah and surveys the party: old ladies, some in bright colors and others in the solid black that counts, among elderly women of all classes, as dressed up.

"Who are they?" she asks the man, deciding to overlook his coarseness. *How did you know I would come? You don't know anything about me!*

"War widows," he answers, "Confederate widows and daughters, if you can believe that."

"Oh." Jenny is amazed. These women are relics. Wasn't the Civil War even before World War I? Yes, it would have to be, because of what she knows about fashion. Hoop skirts came before World War I.

Now, Negro women in white aprons, whom Jenny surmises are attendants or waitresses, move among the Confederate females, who are seated at picnic tables under the oak trees or making their way from table to table, greeting each other. A few old ladies occupy wheelchairs. Many have canes. Their progress is stiff and halting. Won't those big tree roots trip them up? The attendants offer trays of small sandwiches that make Jenny's mouth water. She hasn't eaten anything today. Her apartment was hot when she woke up, as if the pianos and wooden carousel animals were pressing in on her, taking all the air. She can't remember if she has even drunk anything today, water or juice or coffee. She woke feeling lightheaded, almost disoriented.

"What's the occasion?" she asks the man.

"Spring," he says. "They like to have parties here because the place was built by a Confederate soldier. Some of them knew Captain Cussons."

In a low-class way, and seen up close for the first time, this man is incredibly handsome, with black hair and a prowling walk. Even when he's standing still, he seems tense and energetic, as if ready to pounce on her.

"Everybody around here acts so impressed by that old Captain," Jenny says, "even though he's been dead for ages. So what exactly do you do to help at a party like this?"

"They hire me to set up tables and see to the

food," he says.

"What about a regular job? Do you have one?" she asks, and can't believe her ears. She knows better than to interrogate people, but with this man, she'll break all the rules.

He says, "I'm the handyman. As you big-city folks would say, the building supervisor. The super."

"So you fix sinks and things like that?"

"Things like that," he says, and she knows he's mocking her. Is he a gigolo? Shocked, she scans the gathering of old ladies. Many of them are watching her talk with this man. They have even turned their chairs toward them. A few other people join the edges of the gathering, and she imagines they must be tenants of this ancient hotel: a bedraggled woman with a baby, and several old men.

"If you're in charge, then how about getting the whole building painted?" Jenny asks, gesturing to the peeling structure.

"That's not my call," he says. "I don't own the place. Look, you can stay for the party if you want. I have to work."

Jenny rubs her temple as he ambles away. She still feels tired from the walk. She must get a fan for her apartment, or better yet, an air conditioner. There is a Sears Roebuck in Richmond where she can buy fans and air conditioners to her heart's content. Waking in the hot, still air this morning, she had a desire for other things, too, things for Benjamin: striped sheets and a sturdy wooden bed, and a porridge dish like the one she had as a child, with a design of lambs on it. She'll feed Benjamin with a silver spoon engraved with his name. Ideas cascade through her head. This must be what her mother would call a brainstorm. Her best idea was to confront the man who is said to be Benjamin's father, although she hasn't decided what to say to him or what she wants to accomplish.

With effort, she turns her attention to the curious outdoor party. The old ladies seem to know this man. As he makes his rounds, stopping to ask at each table what is needed, he flirts with them, raising one eyebrow, bending his head to catch the sounds of their cracked, throaty voices. He fetches cups of frothy, apricot-colored punch. He retrieves a handkerchief snatched by the breeze, adjusts a black lace shawl around a dowager's hump. The old ladies' excited voices follow him like the tail of a comet. They dart looks at Jenny, and she guesses that this man often has a woman waiting for him, as she is waiting, shameless and idle.

Never mind the antagonism that she felt the first time she laid eyes on him, the day she arrived in Glen Allen. A plan takes shape in her mind. She envisions them as a family: herself and Benjamin and this man whose name she does not even know. This is the man whom Woodrow Johnson identified as their great-grandson's father. Therefore, Jenny and this man and Benjamin should be together. The idea is so firm in her brain that, when she imagines feeding Benjamin from the lamb-painted dish, she can hear Benjamin's handsome, low-class father chuckling nearby, feel his arm brush her sleeve. *We don't have to stay in Glen Allen. We can move to Richmond,* she'll tell the man. *I hear the Fan District is nice. I have some money of my own. Find us a house with a pretty fanlight over the front door. We'll be a family. Our light will shine through the fan-shaped window and people will see that we're happy together. Let's not wait another day!*

Her mother would be so shocked.

"Well, that's one way to get looked at," her mother used to say, observing a white woman with a colored child or a colored man. You never saw it the other way, a white man with a Negro woman out in public, though you saw plenty of Negro women with little light-brown children, so there must be plenty of white men getting together with black women in private. There was a lot of that in Washington, and maybe even more, the farther South you went.

But *he's* white, she argues in her head with her mother, as if she and this man are already a couple. And the baby is special, the baby is Benjamin. It doesn't matter if he is half one and half the other.

Her mother would reel from this, would never admit it into her world.

The man attaches a square wicker basket to himself, a basket with straps that slip over his shoulders, the kind that peanut-sellers use at football games. The basket holds corsages of yellow and pink roses. With a flourish, he gives a corsage to each of the partygoers.

41

There is one corsage left.

"Pin it on me," Jenny commands the man, pushing a shoulder toward him, locking her hands behind her back so that her breasts jut out. The Confederate women buzz like bees to see the man claimed so boldly. As he pins the flower on Jenny's blouse, she holds her breath. Her roses are yellow. Pink would be better for her complexion. Her mother always says yellow flowers make skin look sallow. The man's fingers are warm.

"Ow!" she says as the pin pricks her skin.

"Sorry," he says, but she doesn't think he is. Maybe he wanted to jab her. The skin on his hands looks hard and weatherbeaten, but she can't guess his age.

Then she is startled to realize what day it is. "It's my birthday," she says.

"Is that so," the man says, as if she has revealed a secret about her body.

"I'm twenty-three," she volunteers.

"Happy, happy," he says.

The man steps back, and he and Jenny regard her corsage. Rather, she is looking at the flowers; he is looking only at her breasts. She taps the corsage as if reproving him, and he laughs, showing that he understands. She feels powerful now, flirtatious and in control.

"Did you check her for seam squirrels, Clell?" an old woman calls.

"Mary, hush!" others say. "Don't talk about that."

Jenny raises her head and looks out at the party. The woman who called out is advancing toward them, a stout dinosaur of at least ninety, the one whose shawl the man adjusted on her humped back. Still, the old creature has a proud stance, like a weathered figurehead. "Just playin', darlin'," she says to Jenny. "Seam squirrels, that's what my husband called graybacks."

"I don't understand," says Jenny. The figurehead's breath smells of the apricot punch, ripe and fruity.

"Lice," the dowager hoots. "Graybacks is another name for lice!"

Jenny glares at the old woman and turns to go. She has forgotten why she came here, why she wanted to speak to that arrogant man. With her empty stomach and dry throat, how will she make it home? Why did she walk instead of drive? She has allowed herself to be demeaned by these strangers. *I knew you would come,* he said. In the dark, close silence of her apartment, surrounded by pianos and carousel animals, she will imagine the kind of nights they could have together. She may as well have walked down the road naked and thrown herself at the man's feet.

Another woman approaches her, holding out a plate and a cup. "Honey, you look about famished. Won't you have a bite to eat?" This woman, younger than the others, has a kind face. Jenny pauses and accepts the refreshments.

An almond cookie. A cup of punch. She nibbles and sips. The man—Clell, is it?—moves among the party guests like a groom at a wedding. With surprising strength, the lice-dowager drags a folding chair from a table, offers it to Jenny, and, to Jenny's relief, hobbles away. Jenny sinks into the chair.

The kind-faced woman explains that she is the granddaughter of one of the women. Softly, she says, "You almost fainted. Are you expecting, dear?"

Jenny stares at her, remembering those nighttime multiplication tables with the Topiary.

"I don't think so," she says. Didn't she have a period a couple of weeks ago? She has got to learn to think the way other women think.

"Where is your husband?" the woman asks, indicating Jenny's wedding ring.

"He left me," she says, and as the woman's face melts into pity, a possibility forms in Jenny's mind, the idea that the ghost of the long-ago woman that her husband claimed to see in the Halls' townhouse was something known and familiar to him, something he had witnessed before and knew to obey. The idea lodges in her mind as a truth. She must get away and think it over, get back to her apartment with the carousel animals and follow this thought where it will lead her. But the kind-faced woman won't let her go, and the party surrounding them seems to be growing wilder, cacophonous even.

"Did your husband have another woman?" the woman asks, and Jenny marvels at the nosiness of the question. The woman asks, "Or did he leave because you're in love with Clell?" and nods toward the black-haired figure, compact as a matador among the chattering guests.

When Jenny doesn't answer, the woman says, "It's all right. Keep your secrets, dear. I'm sorry about Mary. She's an embarrassment, talking about lice every chance she gets." The woman pauses and then says, "Let me ask you a favor. Do you use S&H Green Stamps?"

Will this woman never go away? Jenny shakes her head.

"If you don't save them, could I have yours?" the woman asks. "Give them to Clell, and tell him they're for Edith Paylor. That's me. He gives me his. I live just over there," and she points to the woods behind the hotel, which Jenny interprets to mean she lives out on one of the country roads, but not far off.

"I keep all of mine," lies Jenny, not wanting to be bothered with the chore of putting the sticky stamps aside for this woman. During her shopping trips in Richmond, she has gathered enough stamps to fill many booklets, but she just throws them away. They're a nuisance. Her mother gives Green Stamps to the maid and complains that now the maid expects them. So Jenny has learned to avoid the trap of saving S&H Green Stamps for somebody else. The person always gets greedy. She and her mother don't need to save Green Stamps. They can go to any store in Washington and buy what they want, or better yet, just phone and ask for silver candelabra to be wrapped up and sent over, or a half-dozen sets of Wamsutta sheets, or a sterling soup ladle in the Old Master pattern needed at the last minute for a dinner party.

Edith Paylor looks at Jenny in a deep, searching way. "You are very dangerous," she says. "I don't say that as a criticism. But you must know that, already. You've got to. I've heard a little bit about you—the new young woman here. What kind of person goes on vacation with her parents and then stays behind, settles there without her husband? I thought of doing the same thing one time, when my husband and I were on vacation at Buckroe Beach and not getting along. I thought of getting a place of my own and staying there, even when it got cold and the beaches emptied out. I thought about it. I could have sold myself to sailors from the Navy base in Norfolk. That was the only way I could think of to get enough money to survive."

"Do you wish you'd done it?" Jenny says, intrigued now.

"No, but the fact that I almost did it—well, it was something I had, all during those years when I went to PTA meetings and darned my husband's socks and so on. You're the only person I've ever told."

"I won't tell anybody." Still lightheaded, Jenny feels a certain calm. As easily as if requesting a recipe, she asks Edith Paylor, "If you wanted a baby that wasn't your own, how would you go about getting it?"

Edith Paylor regards her for a full minute. "It's

the Johnson child, isn't it? I've seen you go to their house. That little deaf colored baby."

"I want to take care of him."

"Those folks wouldn't take a king's ransom for that child."

With a motion of her head, Jenny indicates the man, Clell, a matador among flowers, leaning down to a picnic table with his arms around two old ladies. She thinks he has forgotten about her until he lifts his head and gazes at her. Desire fills her, sweet and wild.

"I was hoping he could help me," she says, "since it's his child. Did you know that?" She wants to shock this woman, but Edith Paylor doesn't flinch.

Edith Paylor says, "Don't think you can come here and change things. You can't do that."

Tap Dancing

Something makes nine-year-old Shirley Lloyd stop at the piano store one day, a conviction that starts as a distant sound (a mouse, tap dancing?) heard from out on the street, and resolves into the idea, *She needs help. That woman, Jenny, needs help.* Armed with her new glasses—black rectangular frames with a prescription strong enough that she can indeed see people's eyelashes, though never again with the same delight as afforded by Woodrow Johnson's gold spectacles—with these new glasses comes a heightened sense of hearing, as if myopia has lessened Shirley's other senses and she is now reclaiming them. With her restored vision, she can better enjoy the privilege of occasionally walking to school or walking home, rather than taking the bus, a concession her mother has granted now that the school year is almost over. Her sisters still take the bus. Shirley savors the time alone to observe and think.

Standing on the sidewalk in front of the piano

store—BUY SELL TRADE—Shirley doesn't know what, exactly, she hears. When she pushes open the door and steps inside, she hones in further on a faint rapping, deep within the massed furniture. She pictures a mouse in tap shoes spinning, frolicking, sliding down the raised top of a baby grand.

She has seen Jenny a number of times since that morning a few weeks ago in Woodrow Johnson's yard, when she had felt as if Jenny for some reason were angry with her, wished she weren't there, and resented her knowledge of tree rings. Shirley has seen Jenny at the store and has heard talk among her mother's friends of this young woman. Jenny Hall Havener was vacationing here in Glen Allen with her parents, the tale goes, the story that circulates among shoppers at the store, among teachers gossiping during recess. Shirley has gathered (one of her mother's favorite expressions, so discreet: "I have gathered..."), that Jenny liked it here and stayed here, though her parents went back to Washington. Her father actually bought this whole building for her and everything in it, pianos and organs and merry-go-round horses that have been there forever. That would be wonderful, to live in a store instead of a house. Shirley admires Jenny. Ever since Shirley can remember, the piano store has been boarded up, for sale. She has longed to go inside.

And now that is where she is—standing on floors so dusty you can see separate footsteps left by Jenny Hall Havener. The air itself smells like music. How to explain that? It's not the odors of cobwebs or mildew, but glorious dark wood shaped into organs and pianos, and a floral scent of furniture polish, as if long ago, these instruments were loved, as if she is picking up on that, on the hope she would feel if she were a customer, come to choose. *Dulcimer*, she thinks, *harpsichord*. One of the younger teachers at school brought a zither one day and played it for every class, saying her boyfriend had given it to her. The older teachers smiled and frowned simultaneously, an expression that conveyed disdain. No other teachers talk about boyfriends. By frowning and smiling, the older teachers by day's end reduced the zither player to a forlorn outcast, tucking the contraption into its case with jerky, final motions of her hands, as if she and the zither had quarreled.

Shirley pushes the door shut behind her and stands in a wash of spring sunlight. Berry-colored where it hits a piano, the sunshine spreads throughout the room. *I will dream of this*, Shirley thinks. She wonders who stacked the instruments and furniture this way; she searches for the carved animals she has seen through the windows, and yes, there's a wooden horse leaning against a wall, so large that it surely adorned a carousel for giants.

Nobody knows she is here. Her sisters, home by now, her mother, greeting them—they only know she is walking back from school. She knows her mother is waiting for her, anxiously, ready at any moment to revoke Shirley's walks home and to put her back on the school bus, a vehicle that Shirley hates.

Shirley might have ten minutes to do whatever she needs to do here at the mysterious Jenny's place, ten minutes before her mother hops in the car and comes looking for her. Shirley gazes around her, taking stock. If only Shirley could have this place as a kind of giant dollhouse, a playhouse, for herself and her sisters.

"Hello?" Shirley calls into the store. She runs through what else she knows about Jenny: those visits to the Johnsons. Jenny takes them food and presents and then departs, it is said, wiping tears from her eyes. Shirley of course saw Jenny's wild face the day Mr. Johnson gave Shirley the glasses, heard in Jenny's voice the agitation of wanting to see Benjamin.

She's crazy, say the ladies at the store. *Somebody should call her family. Who are her people, anyway?*

Yet Shirley savors the trapped sunlight and the sound of the tap dancing mouse, allowing her ears to trace the noise the way a weathervane responds to a breeze. Her newly sharp hearing zooms in on the mouse: it is performing upstairs, with rapid accomplished steps. Shirley stands still, concentrating. And there comes again the sense of Jenny Hall Havener desperately needing someone, needing Shirley. Making her way to the back of the long room, where the stairs are, Shirley is careful not to touch even one key on the tempting pianos and organs. That would be too easy. These instruments cry out to be played; to touch only a key here or there would be to torment them.

The back of the store loses the light. It's dark with a complicated gloom that reminds Shirley of the sacks of Christmas decorations in Shirley's own attic, the put-away bags of ornaments and tinsel, the wrapped and patient treasures that hoard among them wintry pockets of air even in summertime. Shirley would not be surprised, stumbling upon the Christmas ornaments some August afternoon, to find crusts of snow melting on red metal stars and fiberglass-haired angels.

That Christmas-ornament smell is here too, though it is May and there are no ornaments in sight. Even before Shirley reaches the second story, she divines what she will find: Jenny in trouble, Jenny closed up somehow, trapped and suffocating, beating her knuckles against a door or a lid of some sort.

Shirley will never know how she knew. She races up the steps.

On the second floor, lights are on, and a small table is laid for one, with a plate, silverware, and a water glass set out. An unmade bed occupies a space beneath a window. Everywhere, more organs, pianos, bedsteads, and chests loom in masses, stacked atop each other, so high that Shirley is reminded of a forest. Following the tapping sound with her ears, she creeps forward and discovers, in a space cleared of other furniture, a huge coffin. She freezes while this sinks in. There is logic in a coffin being part of the inventory of a furniture store. She recalls from a history lesson that undertakers used to be cabinet-makers, and vice versa.

She takes a deep breath and kneels down beside the coffin.

"I'm here," Shirley calls and hears for the first time a muffled cry. Her fear is confirmed: Jenny is inside. "I'll get you out," Shirley says, noting the coffin's strong hinges. It must have shut with a bang, forming a tight seal. She will have to pry the lid open, and from there, Jenny will have to help her. From the table, she fetches a dinner knife and wedges it between the lid and the body of the coffin. The knife bends with her effort, but the lid does not lift. She puts the knife aside, her heart pounding, remembering what her father uses to coax stubborn windows open. She pictures the tool, and the name leaps to her lips.

"Have you got a pry bar?" she asks the coffin.

The reply is a high-pitched gibber, fading at the end, as if Jenny has used up the last breath of air inside.

Is there no phone here? Shirley searches around Jenny's apartment. There must be one, but in her panic, she can't find it. "I'll get somebody," she cries to the coffin.

Down the steps she goes, across the vast packed dusty chamber, out the doors, into the street. Waving her arms, calling, "Help, help," she sees nobody. Equidistant from school and home, with houses in between, she is isolated, with Jenny dying in the store. There is no time to run home or back to school where the principal and his secretary are closing up the office for the day. Not a car passes, and the school buses are long since gone.

She goes back inside. She'll have to save Jenny all by herself.

How in the world to get a closed coffin to open? She could try to break it, somehow. She bolts back up the stairs, where the mouse has ceased dancing, where Jenny inside her box might be dead by now.

Shirley leans down to the coffin and says, "I'm going to push you down the stairs."

No answer. At the foot of the coffin, a brass handle is attached, and this she grasps. At first, the coffin doesn't budge, but as Shirley tugs, feeling her neck and jaw muscles strain almost out of her skin, it moves with a sandy sound.

Not a peep from inside. Though sweat trickles into Shirley's eyebrows and eyes, though her new glasses fog up and her chest aches, she doesn't dare stop. She pulls and heaves. The stairs are in sight. The coffin moves more easily now. Her crabbed frenzied steps turn to a gallop as she nears the staircase. The coffin gains momentum as if powered from within. She will have to move aside or plunge headfirst, risking the box's falling on her. She has got to let go.

Let go.

Her fingers are fused with the brass handle; they will not unlock. The coffin, tipping forward on the first step, threatens to tear off her arm. Something in her wrist snaps, but her hand works free just as the coffin pitches downward.

Earthquake. Explosion. Shirley's glasses clap up and down on her nose with every echoing bump. *Boomble-a-boomble-a-bap bap bap!*

Shirley holds her breath. Amid a cloud of dust, the halves of the coffin break open like a cracked pecan, and out pops Jenny, flung through the air like a doll, landing upside down with each limb on a different step. Shirley is relieved to see Jenny's mouth open, gasping. The coffin settles at the bottom of the stairs, busted, beetle-dark and gleaming. Shirley sinks down on the top step, clutching her throbbing wrist, and she and Jenny just stare at each other. Then Shirley, feeling like a nurse or a hostess, or anything except herself, goes in search of a cold cloth and a glass of water for Jenny. It occurs to her that she needs these things, too, but she doesn't stop to get them for herself. When she returns with the cloth and the water, Jenny has righted herself. She reaches for the wet cloth, presses it against her face, and gulps the water.

Jenny's mouth works without sound, and then she says, "It just seemed a shame to live here with all this stuff and not try it out. I sat on the carousel animals. I've tested some of the pianos. You can play them, if you want."

"Okay," Shirley says, though she knows she won't.

She and Jenny sit for a long time, stunned and silent, recovering. Shirley's hurt arm trembles, and she clasps it between her knees.

Then the front door pushes open, and Shirley freezes as if caught in a crime. She can never explain this situation to anybody. Has she done something good, something right? She hears footsteps—a man's. As he draws nearer, panic descends on Shirley. This is how her cats must feel when a stranger approaches. She leaps down the steps and scurries for the door, only to find herself face to face with the black-haired man who lives at the old hotel. Clell, his name is.

His eyes are holes burned in a blanket. He looks amused to see her. "I'm looking for Jenny," he says.

Shirley leads him to the stairs, where Jenny sits above her ruined coffin, mopping her face. Clell goes to the coffin and runs his hand along it. The gesture reminds Shirley of the way in which, on TV soap operas, men touch women's faces. Pay attention to *her*, Shirley wants to say to him, reading Jenny's expression.

"I had to push it down the steps," Shirley tells him, thinking he will demand an explanation. "She didn't have a pry bar."

At this, Clell throws back his head and laughs. *Threw back his head* — for the first time in her life, Shirley will speak this phrase aloud, if she tells everything to her mother. She'll have to, because of her wrist. She won't tell how glorious it was to make a man, this man, laugh, but the phrase will give that away.

"What were you doing in there?" Clell asks Jenny.

Jenny smiles—a crooked smile, thinks Shirley. Jenny says, "I wanted to see if it was comfortable. I thought I'd read or take a nap, so I put a pillow in there." She points to a burgundy cushion in the wreckage of the coffin. "Then bang, the lid came down. I couldn't lift it, so I kept knocking. See? My knuckles are all sore."

"How long were you in there before she came along?" Clell asks, indicating Shirley.

"I don't know," says Jenny, and Shirley thinks she should leave now, right this instant, so Jenny and this man can be alone. Shirley was in Jenny's way at Mr. Johnson's house, and she's in her way again, never mind that she saved Jenny's life.

Clell asks Jenny, "Were you running out of air?"

"God, yes," says Jenny. "I almost died. I don't ever want to think about that again."

Shirley becomes aware of a smell, a cedary, churchy scent that must be from the coffin itself, from the split wood, jagged along the hinges, a smell as pungent as a curse, as sudden as a dead person's rising. What kind of wood is it? Mr. Johnson would know.

"She saved my life," says Jenny, in a voice that Shirley realizes is meant only for Clell. Shirley is already superfluous to her. "Listen," says Jenny. "When I was in—there—I remembered something my dad told me a long time ago. There was this old cemetery, and the graves had to be dug up and moved. One of the, uh, caskets broke open when they picked it up, and you know what was in it?"

"What?" asks Clell.

"A bride," says Jenny triumphantly, mopping the back of her neck with the cloth, which Shirley thinks must be warm by now. "A bride, and she'd been buried alive. They knew because the veil was wrapped round and round her. She'd turned over, trying to get out."

"Did your dad actually see that?" asks Clell.

"He told me about it, so I guess he did," says Jenny.

Shirley takes this in, fascinated.

Lightly, Clell tips up the steps toward Jenny. When he nears her, she swats his backside, playful and familiar. Shirley knows they have forgotten she is there.

"Just call me your little adrenaline junkie," Jenny tells Clell.

Shirley will look up "adrenaline" and "junkie" in her mother's dictionary. "I have to go home," she says.

Nobody stops her. She finds herself outside in the daylight, where the afternoon has resumed. Did she dream the whole episode? A car passes and then another one, a dog trots across the street, and a warm, blossomy smell lifts from a weedy plot behind Jenny's building, making Shirley think of summer, of flower names that she loves: dusty miller, yarrow, cosmos.

Of course she will dwell on the bride in Jenny's story, the bride whose veil was her winding sheet, herself and her veil both spider web and fly.

A car pulls up beside Shirley, her mother's car. Her mother leans over and motions Shirley in. Because of her injured wrist, Shirley will have to tell her mother what happened, at least the bare outlines of saving Jenny. She might even tell about the sound of a dancing mouse, and still there will be enough of the adventure to keep to herself.

The Iguana That Was Our Friend

JENNY MOVES AS IF SHE IS IN A DREAM. BRUISED all over, she has never felt better in her life. The bruises bloom tan and royal blue. There is relief, honesty, in the discomfort. All she has to do is touch her hip or tilt her head, and there it is, pain.

If the casket had not been a fancy one, lined and padded and quilted inside, why, she would probably be dead from the way it tumbled over on the steps. She would definitely be dead if Shirley Lloyd hadn't happened to come by. Yet she still doesn't like that child.

The day of the coffin, she had thought Shirley Lloyd would never leave. The child was intruding upon her time with Clell, who showed up as if summoned. The experience of nearly dying and of being saved, of bursting out of the coffin as if reborn, has made Jenny feel sexy and confident and witty. When she and Clell were at last alone, they went up to her bed, made love, and fell asleep. This was what making love was supposed to be, the yearning of it, the wanting and the satisfaction of it, so much finer than mere multiplication tables. Later, when they woke up, she offered to fix him something to eat, but he wouldn't stay. She accepted that. While he put his clothes on, she lay on the bed, watching him, wanting to say Benjamin, bring me Benjamin, but not daring that much, not yet. She knows so little about Clell, after all, only that he is the most magnetic man she has ever known. The fact that he fathered a child with a Negro woman only makes him seem more bohemian.

When he was gone, she made herself a ham sandwich and wandered through her strange home. She was naked except for her bathrobe. How could she feel so rested, after this day? Moving up and down the stairs, through the cavernous rooms of pianos and organs, she imagined she would walk forever through this soft spring night, alone.

Now, she steps outside. There is nobody around, and the air is so warm and lovely she might be asleep and dreaming. She wishes she could talk to somebody. Edith Paylor had pointed past the old hotel, saying, *I live over there*. Jenny hesitates, wondering if she would enjoy a visit with Edith Paylor, then remembers the nosiness and the business about Green Stamps and thinks not. She has almost reached the railroad tracks before she realizes she is still in her bathrobe, with nothing underneath, walking out in public, barefoot. She can't really remember walking to the tracks. She leans down and touches the rails. She was right here with her parents, yet that earlier self is gone.

She hurries back to BUY SELL TRADE. Nobody saw her leave, and nobody sees her return. She washes her scratched feet and goes to bed. In the morning, her sheets are covered with little spots of blood, where her feet must have kept on bleeding.

§

Being with Benjamin becomes even more painful than not being with him, because the separations have become unbearable, times to be absolutely dreaded. When Jenny is with Benjamin, she wraps her arms around him, and her sobs are howls of grief. Hattie Johnson permits daily visits of an hour or two. If Jenny gets too loud, crying and carrying on, Hattie banishes her to the yard, without Benjamin. There's nothing to do out there except count the rings on that stupid stump and take down the wash from the line. Jenny does this competently, mechanically, folding sheets and towels, shirts and aprons all smelling of sunshine and clean air, rolling into pairs the thick gray socks, knitted by Hattie, worn by both Hattie and Woodrow. Only when Jenny calms down is she readmitted to the house. On days when Woodrow Johnson is not out on his tinker rounds, he sleeps. Jenny understands he has a job guarding an old lady's property at night.

Hattie Johnson refuses to let Jenny take Benjamin out of the house. "He stay here," she replies to Jenny's requests for outings. For emphasis, she turns her broom upside down and taps the floor with the handle. Benjamin's eyes stretch wide, seeking

Jenny's face. He can't hear the raps, but he feels the motion through the floor.

What she wouldn't give to hear him make any kind of sound, to say even one word. He never does. It's as if there is no speaking mechanism in his throat.

Only Hattie or Woodrow may take Benjamin out into the yard. He is toilet trained, and Jenny is relieved to discover that the Johnsons do have a rudimentary indoor bathroom, rather than an outhouse. Hattie does not allow Jenny to bathe Benjamin, dress him, or help him eat. Jenny may, however, play games that she and Benjamin devise together, involving matchboxes, marbles, and an old lantern that she guesses to be still in occasional use, though the house has electricity. Jenny may not strike matches, and she must demonstrate to Hattie that the lantern is empty of oil. This is galling.

Jenny brings Benjamin expensive, glorious toys from shops in Richmond, but Hattie picks over the bags and boxes and accepts only crayons, paper, and, hesitating, a G.I. Joe. "Take 'em on back," she says of Frisbees, Slinkys, model airplane kits, a child-sized football uniform and helmet, and a space suit. As if Jenny has brought garbage into the house, Hattie shakes her head over Play-Doh, an Easy-Bake Oven, an Etch-a-Sketch, a Magic Slate, and a parachute man. Hattie's lips are pressed into a tight line.

"Why don't you just keep them? Put them away till he's older," Jenny suggests, her heart pounding.

She is terrified of this woman. "I guess some of this stuff is for older children, isn't it, but what about this?" She holds up a box containing a miniature barnyard, complete with tiny cows, chickens, and horses. There is a farmer who almost looks colored, with a dark plastic face.

"He have everything he need. This is too much extra," Hattie says. "He a baby."

"Oh, but he's growing. Our little boy's getting big!" Jenny says, afraid her words sound like a taunt. She routinely measures Benjamin against the doorway between the kitchen and the cluttered adjacent room that other people might call a living room but which the Johnsons use for all kinds of work—Hattie's ironing board is in there, and Woodrow's tools. During the time Jenny has known Benjamin, he has grown, though in fact only a little.

"I could have a swing set built in your yard," Jenny offers, "and wouldn't he like a tricycle?"

Hattie shakes her head.

"A puppy? I can get a real gentle one, or a kitten. Oh, come on, Hattie," Jenny dares to say, wishing she had her mother's authoritative way with Negroes, "every child wants a pet."

"No."

When did Hattie stop calling her ma'am, being deferential the way she was the day Jenny first met them? Now she's haughty Hattie, dismissing Jenny's largesse as if chasing away Santa Claus. Besides the crayons, paper, and G.I. Joe, the only gift that has been tolerated is the atomizer which Jenny's mother bought at the Homestead gift shop. It rests on the Johnsons' table beside a Morton salt box. Benjamin loves to squeeze the bulb and send out a fine spray of water. Hattie has poured out the perfume that came with it, rinsing it so that only the faintest scent remains, a hint of lily-of-the-valley that makes Jenny miss her mother.

It would be futile to ask the Johnsons what they would take for Benjamin. Put so baldly, Jenny's request would horrify them. They might have her arrested. She would be denied all access to Benjamin. Maybe one day, Benjamin himself will ask his great-grandparents if he can live with Jenny. The fact that Benjamin never speaks does not prevent Jenny from hoping. When she talks with him, his face gives signs of understanding her, and he's always glad to see her. He puts his arms around her neck and snuggles close. Jenny lives for those moments.

"My beloved," she whispers to him, at the Johnsons' kitchen table. "Precious baby angel." Hattie cleans the stove and mops the floor. Jenny lifts her feet so Hattie can wash beneath the table. Any day, Jenny expects the Johnsons to bar her from the house. She sees no indication that they are using the groceries that she heaps upon them, fine foods sent by delivery truck, but she doesn't dare ask, *Where's the turkey I sent and the devil's food cake and the fresh vegetables?* She had a new bicycle delivered to Woodrow Johnson, a sleek

Schwinn from a Richmond sporting goods store, but he keeps on riding his old one. She believes the Schwinn to be in the backyard shed, perhaps along with the groceries, the bike with its oiled chain and perfect tires going to waste, the food rotting and spoiling, unless they eat it at night and throw away every bone and pit so she won't have the pleasure of seeing the results of her generosity. The old colored people defy her, madden her, hold her hostage with her love for Benjamin. Not knowing the rules of the game they are playing, Jenny deduces only that she has not yet lost; she has daily time with Benjamin. She challenges them, showing up earlier and earlier, finally one day at dawn.

And this is so early that she actually catches Woodrow Johnson as he glides home like an owl on his rusty bicycle from his protecting-the-old-lady job. Night is just ending. Never before has Jenny been awake this early. But she is up and dressed and in the Johnsons' yard, her hand raised to knock on the door.

Woodrow wheels to a stop, dismounts, and murmurs a greeting. He, at least, is still polite to her. She steps aside so he can open his door. She wonders just what his job involves. Dozing on the front porch of the old lady's house, strolling around her property? Jenny has heard talk of vandals blowing up mailboxes. Well, if they're just kids, she supposes Woodrow can chase them off. Woodrow squeezes past Jenny and pushes the door open, and there's Hattie, coffee pot in hand, fresh bandana around her head, as if she's been up all night, as if she never needs to sleep. Woodrow vanishes into the house.

"Not yet," Hattie says and blocks the door as Jenny peers into the room for Benjamin. "He not awake. You have to wait."

Jenny settles on the stump in the yard, consoled by a cup of black coffee Hattie hands her through the door. She remembers getting chiggers at camp one summer from sitting on an old log. Hastily, she rises, smoothing her skirt, wishing she had worn shorts instead. It is June, and the days are warm and balmy, even the early mornings.

She can go no farther. She can't leave this yard. It's too early for laundry on the line, and there are no chairs, so she strolls back and forth, tagging the road with the toe of her shoe. She watches a bumblebee explore Woodrow Johnson's bike, crawling and buzzing over the handlebars and the ancient metal implements that he uses to repair, she supposes, scissors and pots. His customers must be very poor. Otherwise, wouldn't they just throw away their dull scissors and broken pans? She feels the futility of giving the Johnsons anything more, ever. She could commission the invention of a pot-repairing machine so that he could repair the faulty cookware of the entire Commonwealth of Virginia. Yet all of that would get her not one moment more with Benjamin. She hates the Johnsons' fortitude, their proud poverty, their hardihood, the *don't-need-nothing* spirit of their lives. She hears the singsong phrase in her mind, though they have never spoken it to her. They are so smug. Anger makes her hand sweat on her empty cup. The idea of pots brings back a memory. During her brief time in college, she had to read a story about a tinker and some pots of chrysanthemums. There was something about a woman who was sad, who wanted to drink wine, and somehow the tinker tricked her, did something bad to her. The chrysanthemums were thrown away, and Jenny's teacher claimed that the empty pots were a symbol of sexual frustration. Other students nodded sagely, but Jenny felt nettled and bored. She pushes the story from her mind.

The Johnsons have no right to act so proud. Weren't they slaves, not that long ago? Or their parents, at least. Maybe not. There used to be black people who were not only free, but rich. Jenny imagines Hattie in a pompadour and crinoline, presiding over a silver tea service, Benjamin at her knee, Jenny ever an interloper, someone who can be waved away.

The sun sails higher, a shifting light in a pearl-gray sky. It occurs to her that she could go close enough to the house to see through the open window, to see if Woodrow Johnson is really asleep after his night at work. Edging closer, carefully, Jenny becomes a vine, a creeper, gaining so gradually on the side of the house that nobody will notice. Close, closer, she reaches the sill, but it's dark in the room, as if Woodrow took the night inside with him. Shading her eyes, she leans down and gazes through the screen.

Inside, a thin electric light shines across what she realizes is a table or a desk next to a window, and there sits Woodrow, writing. The top of his head is just inches from her face. The screen is pocked with holes where insects probably enter. One hole is so big, she could stick her fingers through it. Woodrow's hand moves rapidly across a sheet of paper. Okay. She can give them some decent stationery, monogrammed. She will need to find out his middle initial and his favorite color, so that she can pick out a stylish ensemble of vellum cards and envelopes. She could bring home the color samples from the printer, but that would give him a chance to refuse. Maybe he would enjoy sealing wax, too. She loved sealing wax as a child; she had different colors of wax and several beautiful brass seals, which made designs when pressed into the hot wax. Or maybe he'd like a typewriter, a heavy-duty electric Smith-Corona. Pens by Parker. Or Cross. Who on earth does he write to, and about what?

Woodrow lifts his head. "You messing up my light," he says.

He reaches up and yanks down the shade with a ripping sound. Jenny cries out, her breath sticking in her throat as she retreats.

There is nowhere to put her coffee cup except the stump.

Darting about on the stump is a salamander, a tiny brown lizard with a blue tail. Jenny hunts it. She squats beside the stump and stalks it, reaching lightning-fast for the slim scurrying body, the blazing tail.

There is nothing to do but wait and remember.

She and her mother were never so close as in the days of Iggy, the iguana or gecko or whatever he was. Oh, Iggy said such outrageous things. Jenny, a teenager at the time, and her mother spoke in first person, as if both were Iggy. They used funny voices. Iggy talked crudely about sex, men's "ding-dongs" and such. Jenny and her mother had never had so much fun. Iggy mocked everybody they knew. Jenny and her mother passed hilarious hours this way, until their lips stiffened from the effort of speaking in Iggy's reedy, cynical voice. Up and down the stairs of the Washington townhouse, as they went through their days, they would break into Iggy-talk, passing a deadpan reedy remark so suddenly that it sent both of them into convulsions of laughter. Even after Iggy was dead, the talk continued for a while. From the tomb, Iggy made his trademark caustic observations about their friends and relatives. National tragedies revived him. He was politically astute. The day of Kennedy's assassination, he was downright garrulous, out of earshot of Jenny's father. Iggy talked about the girls Kennedy had had, women with whom he'd betrayed Jackie. Shocked, fascinated, Jenny had wondered where all that was coming from. Even her father, a Senate staff member, didn't know all of that.

Her mother doesn't seem to remember. Last time they spoke on the phone, Jenny made a comment in the Iggy voice, and her mother said Jenny didn't sound at all like herself, was she getting a cold? Jenny has begun telling her mother lies—that she is making friends here, that neighbors have invited her to supper.

Her husband—and yes, a voice tells her, as if chiding her for the silly nickname, he is not the Topiary, he is your husband—must have hated all of it, the entire life he was living with her and her parents. If Jenny's parents were here, they would be taking pictures of her as she chased the salamander. She would be forced to reenact the poses that pleased them, bending over the stump, reaching for the elusive reptile. Her parents must have fifty photo albums. For the first time in her life, Jenny questions the family habit of pointing to the side whenever pictures are taken. She and her parents remind each other, "Point!" as if there is something enchanting just beyond, something extraordinary that others will never see. In picture after picture, the Halls point triumphantly, to suggest some involvement beyond themselves. It maddens her, thinking of how her parents would make her point to the side, if they were with her at this stump. Point!

You don't have to do that anymore, comes Iggy's voice in her mind.

There's the salamander again. She grabs but misses, pricking her fingertip on a splinter in the stump. Oh, Benjamin would love a salamander. She could keep it in her pocket and show it to him, and

Hattie need never know. Its bright eyes would blink from the depths of her pocket, a secret that she and Benjamin would share. What if she hurts it, in catching it? What if it bit her? What would Hattie do if Jenny rushed to the door waving a bloody reptile, a bleeding hand? Jenny laughs creakily. The salamander vanishes into a crack in the stump. She slumps back on her behind, then remembers chiggers again and stands up.

Mourning doves call, sounding as lonely as she feels. It's still early, so early that in her old life, in Washington, she would just be getting out of bed, pushing at the curlers in her hair. So sheltered she has been, she might have lived like Iggy in a terrarium, dozing through her days. That life is slipping away from her. Now her real life is the store with the pianos and carousel horses and the nights when Clell appears, like a magician or an intruder, for he does not knock. He does not need to, because she leaves BUY SELL TRADE unlocked, for him. Lightly, he pads up the stairs to her living quarters and puts his arms around her waist. How old are you? she has asked him, and he says, a hundred and thirty-nine.

He never talks about Benjamin. That is a rule: she must not, either. He made that clear, the one time she even said Benjamin's name. He does not ever want to be in the role of a father, he has said, not to anyone, and certainly not to a little Negro boy. *But*, she says, and he places his hand over her mouth. The hand is warm and leathery like a cat's paw, smelling like a cat's foot, used and oily and pleasant. Shh, Clell says.

Benjamin lives in her brain in a room all his own, on a throne she has made for him, hung with golden curtains. She tells the carousel horses about Benjamin, but they already know; their painted wooden faces and elegant stance bear witness to an ancient awareness of Benjamin, of how it feels to love. She has spoken to them of Benjamin in halting low phrases, putting her hand on their carved curving necks, the sculpted manes, the faces with deeply socketed eyes painted blue and green and gold. Some have tails shaped like waves, others like cornichons, those tightly furled seashells with a hidden creature inside. She has stood in the gloom of her apartment and believed that carved circus animals understand more about her heart than anybody else ever will.

The Johnsons' yard is growing hotter and more humid. Jenny's skin itches, and too late, she hears the thin whine of a mosquito. She flicks the mosquito from her arm, but it has already stung her. Oh, pests and plagues: she recalls a long-ago friend launching into a story about contracting scabies from a pet hamster. The girl had held up her arms, demonstrating tiny scars, her expression horrified. Jenny remembers the girl's face and the shape her arms made as she lifted them, but she can't remember what scabies is. Like rabies? Iggy would have had a wisecrack about it. She wonders what prompted that memory. She can whisper all of that to Benjamin and wait to see the light in his eyes that means he understands. His gums are sunset caves with tiny teeth. When he clicks his teeth, can he hear that sound in his head? Had Jenny, the younger girl-Jenny, made any response to the scabies story, sensible or otherwise? Oh, it's good to be grown.

All she wants is to walk with Benjamin, to take him out on the long strolls she has begun on her own, hours'-long excursions in which she imagines he is with her. She loses track of time, of place. She has knocked on doors to ask, where am I? Startled housewives have directed her back to Mountain Road. Sometimes she walks with her eyes closed, on empty, unpaved paths. At least she remembers to wear shoes now. She might follow the train tracks, going deeply into fields of yellow flowers, waving at the train, thinking, I will disappear. If she has to pee, she finds a place in the trees. Benjamin would glory in these adventures. She pictures them together in the Fall, on a rapturous walk through broom sedge gold with afternoon light. His deafness would not matter. Who needs to hear, when there is all this other? Only once was she afraid, when she was surrounded by a pack of stray dogs. They came out of nowhere. She was out in the open, near the railroad tracks, and the dogs mobbed her, growling and dancing close, four or five mongrels with fire in their eyes, ready to leap on her and eat her from the throat down, the ankles up. Keep walking, said a voice in her head, and she did, imagining she held Benjamin close, bearing him through this, comforting him. Finally the dogs scattered, snapping at each other, chasing off. Sometimes, her head hurts, and then she feels so tired that she lies down in a field and naps. She wakes up thirsty but happy, knowing it will soon be the next day and time for a visit with Benjamin.

Jenny has so much to say to Clell, but he doesn't like to talk.

She does not love Clell. She is careful not to fall asleep before he does. The dream of the fanlight is gone, the house with a fanlight where the three of them might live. She has come a long way, to leave that picture behind, and to survive the wait in the Johnsons' yard. Hattie must be watching her. Hattie will see that Jenny's back is straight, her shoulders squared, her blouse crisp and clean, her nails painted, though the grooming rituals seem more and more foreign, the Washington clothes like costumes, and her hair is growing out from the style achieved by the sad-eyed beautician at The Homestead back on that spring day of snow.

Benjamin is worth this. As soon as she holds him, as soon as she smells the top of his head, she will know joy.

She has been in this yard so long, is it even the same day as when she set out? She knows every inch of grass by heart. The salamander appears and locks eyes with her, and she reaches out fast enough to brush its tail before it disappears.

What about a phone? Would the Johnsons like

a phone? She can offer that. If they want a white, princess-style phone just like hers, she'll get them one. She'll call the phone company and make all the arrangements, after checking with Hattie first, of course.

But it's Sunday. The phone company is closed.

If she were in Washington, she'd be having waffles for breakfast, and then she and her parents would go to the Episcopal church. Why has she never seen the Johnsons going to church? Aren't all colored people supposed to be religious? They're supposed to spend their whole day worshipping, and Sunday nights too, plus Wednesday nights, singing hymns and calling out to Jesus, egging on their preacher as he gets worked up and wild, "Rip the cover off it, Reveren'!" What is the matter with the Johnsons, that they don't go? There's some satisfaction in this: she has found a flaw. Jenny bets Jesus would agree, that He would have some things to say about the Johnsons, especially Hattie. Jenny listens, and in her mind she hears Jesus's voice, which sounds like Iggy's, like Iggy mocking a colored person: *She no saint, she just a mean ol' woman, mean ol' gal with a rag round her head, she don't suffer herself to come to Me. She gone get a surprise when them flames start a-licking her, those hell flames gone be mighty hot on her bunions and corns, fanning her ass, she gone wish she'd been nicer to Jenny then, uh huh!*

Jenny laughs out loud, and the sound dies away in the scruffy yard.

The Johnsons' neighbors appear to live in sheds,

rough structures once painted pink or purple, from which men or women or children occasionally emerge to be glimpsed, but not today. Maybe nobody in this whole neighborhood goes to church. But it's still early, just past seven, by Jenny's watch. Oh, how long must she wait out here? Talking with Jesus is tiresome; anything but being with Benjamin is like buying your soul, over and over. Are they going to leave her out here all day? Who are the others that Benjamin has charmed, just by being himself? "He do people that way," Hattie said, early on, and now the idea of rivals is a torment, the idea of others smitten and besotted with him. Maybe they, too, these faceless competitors, are allotted their precious time with him, their measured hours and minutes doled out by Hattie, and they are succeeding, winning him, winning all of the Johnsons.

Her whole being is attuned to the weathered door, at which after an hour and forty-four minutes by Jenny's watch, Hattie appears, not waving, not speaking, just flashing her impassive face at Jenny, who moves toward her, clutching the empty coffee cup.

She's far gone and she knows it. If the entire neighborhood ridiculed her, if the whole world jeered and mocked her, if the Topiary rode up and told the Johnsons about his dissatisfaction with their multiplication tables, she would bear it, all the humiliation that could be heaped upon her, would crawl over knives to reach that door.

Everything Must Go

GLEN ALLEN IS SLEEPING, EXCEPT FOR JENNY. On her long walks through short streets of houses and country roads of fields and small farms, Jenny observes the effects of enchantment: people and animals, beguiled, sleepwalking through their days. In finding Benjamin, she has left behind all pettiness, all her old worries, and though she has new worries, she also has dreams, for the first time in her life, dreams of days with Benjamin, teaching him, helping him grow up. She stops by the railroad tracks and rubs her eyes, which feel tired and strained, and she is overcome with emotion.

Thank goodness she has these long walks, for otherwise, how would she fill the hours without him? Hattie has begun shortening her visits. Hattie will say, "It's time for his nap," earlier all the time, and then she waits at the door until Jenny leaves.

Finally, Jenny confronts her. "Are you mad with me because I'm a friend of Clell's? You don't let me visit very long, any more."

Hattie answers, "I said nap time. That's what."

"I'm good to Benjamin, aren't I?" Jenny demands. "You have to admit that." She's near tears, but she can't break the rule she has made for herself: don't lose control.

"Nap time," Hattie says, holding the door open for Jenny to leave.

So, the walks.

The old hotel is an eye always watching her. Not Clell, but the hotel itself, its tall towers: eyes. Clell might be a sleepwalker. And that child, Shirley Lloyd, she's sleepwalking even though she did save Jenny's life, and so are Hattie and Woodrow Johnson.

Jenny takes down the BUY SELL TRADE sign in the window of her home and hangs up a homemade sign saying ALL ITEMS FREE. EVERYTHING MUST GO.

It's an impulse, but irresistible. Clearing out the furniture, the musical instruments, all of it, will be a relief. That way, she'll never wind up in a coffin again, not while she's alive. And there's something else, too: the painted horses with their big round eyes had seemed at first to understand her, to sympathize with her love for Benjamin, but now the horses' gaze is cold. She wants them to go away. She puts a second sign in her window, in case people think the first one is just a joke.

A week passes, as if nobody has noticed or as if they don't believe it. Then people trickle in, skeptical, giddy. The pianos and organs are the first to go. Local schools and churches take those, and a few individuals and families. Jenny asks no questions, discourages conversation. Cemetery representatives show up with a truck, and they cart away the coffins, even the broken one that Jenny got stuck in.

One night, a van pulls up, and from her second-floor apartment, she hears grunts and creaks down below. She holds her breath, knowing if whoever is downstairs decides to come up and harm her, there would be little that she could do. Fear makes her veins feel electric, almost the way she feels when she's in bed with Clell.

In the quiet, sunlit morning, she goes downstairs and finds that all the carousel horses are gone. She has been robbed by strangers, and she did nothing to stop it.

"Goodbye," she tells the empty space, and her voice echoes. The noise in the night had frightened her, but now there's just a dusty floor and faded walls. There is glory in not keeping track, in not caring; she can't describe it, does not want to share these feelings with anybody except Benjamin. She sits on the stairs for a long time, with the sense that the whole day might be passing. She can do that these days, sit or walk for hours without hunger or tiredness or any feeling at all.

Much later, Clell strolls in, looks around with wide eyes, and says, "You gave away a fortune."

"You sound like my mother," she says. "Besides, you knew I was going to. You saw the sign. I had the sign in the window for days."

Those wooden horses were always watching her, like the towers on the old hotel. The horses and the towers have watched her on her long walks, as she lay down for naps in strangers' fields, as she rubbed her eyes beside the train tracks.

"All that stuff was in the way. And it was mine to give," she says. "To give away."

She could have burned it all, but that would have been too much trouble. Her head is aching again. Sex cures headaches. She read that in a racy magazine. She hurries down the stairs to Clell and gives him the smile that means she is his, for an hour or two. But a throb of pain makes her put her hand to her head. For a moment, the pain takes her breath away.

"Are you sick?" Clell asks.

"I keep getting headaches," she says.

"The man who lived here a long time ago, who had this store, got sick and died," Clell says.

"So what? Was he old? I'm not going to die."

"All the water in Glen Allen still comes from wells. There's arsenic is some of them, flowing from arsenic springs, or at least, there used to be."

"Do you mean I'm drinking poison?" Jenny asks.

"Just listen," Clell says. "Back when the old hotel was a resort, Captain Cussons had the springs tested by chemists. You can still find some of the springs on the grounds, if you know where to look. Alum, lithia, sulphur, arsenic. People used to think arsenic in water was healthy. The grounds of the hotel used to come all the way out to this property. Supposedly, the arsenic spring was capped off, but I've always wondered. If I were you, I'd get your water checked."

She stares at him. It's the longest speech she has ever heard him make. "Well, the water's fine here," she says. It runs out of the taps in the sink and the tub cold and clear. Maybe this means he cares about her, would be sorry if she died from poisoned water. "Listen. You've got to help me, Clell," she says, "help me get Benjamin. I can take better care of him than those old people, and you're his father. We should be together, all three of us. I have money of my own in the bank, and we could..."

His hand is over her mouth, hard, but she steps away from him and says, "It's driving me crazy, don't you see? I love that little boy. He ought to belong to me."

"That's your problem. That child is nothing to me. I'm not even sure I'm the father. What do you plan to do, kidnap him?"

When she doesn't answer, he says, "You're on your own. I won't help you do anything like that."

"Can you at least tell me about his mother?" Jenny begs, hating the way she sounds. "Old Hattie says it's her granddaughter Lois."

Clell's face is dark, unreadable.

Jenny asks, "What happened to her? How did she die?" Again to Jenny's mind comes the image of the unknown Lois in a red dress, enticing men in a bar.

As if reading her thoughts, Clell says, "Men were fighting over her. She was killed in the crossfire."

"Oh." Jenny is conscious of a kind of envy in her heart, envy of a woman so attractive that men would shoot each other for her. "Was she beautiful?"

Clell nods. "She was."

"And is Benjamin her only child?"

"As far as I know. Look, Jenny, in my opinion, you're nuts. If you don't start thinking about something else, you'll flip your lid."

Flip your lid. Such a funny expression, worthy of Iggy. Jenny laughs. She reaches toward Clell and puts her arms around his neck. "Why did you come over here? To see how nuts I've gotten?" This would make five times, she thinks, five times they've climbed the stairs and headed for her bed.

Clell stands still. At last, he unhooks her hands from his neck. "Not today," he says. "I'll see you around."

She is desperate. "Clell," she says. "Do you know anybody who could do me a favor? I need a man who could put on a doctor uniform and go to the Johnsons' house and tell them he's taking Benjamin to the hospital. Do you have any friends who could do that? I'll pay."

"Do you realize what you're saying? No, Jenny."

"You won't tell anybody, will you? If I do something, if I go away, you won't tell anybody what we talked about?" Jenny asks.

He studies her face for a long time. Now she doesn't want him. She only wants to return to the

Johnsons' ragged yard, knock on their door, and be with Benjamin. She'll think of something, some way to be with him forever.

At last, Clell says, "Okay, I won't tell anybody, but quit trying to rope me in to your plans."

"Don't you feel anything for him? He's your son, after all. Your son, Clell."

"I told you I won't talk about him." Clell turns and walks away.

"Wait a minute," Jenny calls, following him. "You can at least answer that, Clell." But he keeps on going, slipping out the door, and this enrages her. She hurries after him. He's getting in his car, a jalopy, just the kind of thing a low-class man would drive.

"You think you're something," she yells. "Well, you're nothing. You're nobody."

She wishes there were somebody to see them, to take her side. Clell drives away. With a start, she looks up at the sky and finds that it's dark out, and all around her, there is quiet, the silence of bedtime, of families and old people and animals dropping off to sleep. She doesn't think she ate anything today. She sits down on the broken sidewalk in front of her building.

For an hour, maybe two, she sits there, thinking hard. The moon rises. An idea is coming to her, something important. She sits very still, and at one point, she feels the tiny legs of an insect exploring her bare arm. A daddy longlegs climbs up her elbow. She gently blows it from her skin. The road smells peppery. Not a single car goes by, not one.

Eye, Ear, Nose, and Throat

"WE HAVE TO GET BENJAMIN TO A DOCTOR, Hattie," Jenny says. "I made an appointment with the best ear specialist in Richmond."

Jenny has Benjamin in her arms and the car keys in her hand. It's morning. She's counting on the element of surprise, making an early strike. Hattie is supposed to clean one of the churches today. Jenny won't take no for an answer. Hattie's rejection of an Etch-a-Sketch is one thing, rejection of a doctor quite another.

Hattie sits at the table, drinking coffee from a bowl, deliberately taking her time.

"I'll have him back as soon as possible," Jenny says and turns to go. She resists the urge to run with Benjamin to her car. He has gained weight, she's glad to notice, and is trusting and relaxed in her grasp.

Her last remark, of course, is a lie. She will never bring him back, for today is the day she has waited for, the day she will take him away with her. After much thought, she has abandoned her idea of trying to hire someone to impersonate a doctor and decided on a visit to a real one, after which she will take Benjamin out of the office, out of Richmond forever. She has not decided where they will go, but she knows that an answer will come to her at the right time. She will decide on a destination only when she has him away from Hattie, so that Hattie can't read her mind or pry any information out of her.

"Of course, I am going too," Hattie says, setting down the bowl and wiping her lips with a napkin. Then she pours herself another bowl of coffee, stirring in sugar and adding a generous splash of cream. The milkman's twice-weekly visits, courtesy of Jenny, have been accepted, and Jenny has to remind herself not to remark on the Johnsons' obvious enjoyment of this new plentitude of dairy products. She must avoid seeming self-congratulatory.

"Don't you have to work today?" Jenny asks. "Aren't you supposed to clean a church?"

"I can do that tomorrow just as well as today," Hattie says. She sips her coffee.

This second bowl of coffee is too much. Jenny would like to leave the old woman sitting there. This idle drinking of the rich coffee, each sip a punishment to Jenny, is maddening. Jenny stares at the container of cream, hardly seeing it. Curles Neck Dairy, it says, with a picture of a smiling cow amid flowers, and Jenny's breath is tight with anger. If Hattie goes for a third bowl of coffee, Jenny will fly right on out the door with Benjamin, and Hattie be damned.

Jenny will not be thwarted. She will even put up with Hattie for a good part of the day: after they visit the doctor, she can treat them all to lunch at the Clover Room, famous for its ice cream, and after that, she will find the right moment to carry Benjamin with her, away from Hattie. She has dressed carefully in a starched white blouse and petal-pink skirt for what is likely to be a long day of travel. In her pocketbook is an envelope containing five thousand dollars in cash, withdrawn by wire from the bank in Washington, DC where she has an account. In the trunk of her car is a suitcase packed with essentials, just in case there is not time to stop at BUY SELL TRADE. The thought of being on the run is exciting. She will certainly have to be out of Virginia by nightfall, though she does not believe the police will look very hard for a Negro, especially not a child. Hattie might report him missing, kidnapped, but she and Woodrow will have little power; a case such as this will barely rate a mention in the paper. If Jenny is stopped and questioned, she will say that she rescued the child from a bad situation. And wouldn't people believe her, rather than Hattie?

She has no idea if the doctor she called is good or not; she found him in the Yellow Pages. But it sounds more impressive, more authoritative, to tell Hattie that he is the best in town. Benjamin after all deserves the best. Jenny has never been able to get a straight answer from Hattie about how closely Benjamin has been examined by previous physicians, if any. She bets he's never been seen. Indignation makes her fearless.

"Well, hurry up, then," she tells Hattie.

With ponderous dignity, Hattie rises from the table, fetches an ancient pocketbook from a hook on the wall, and follows Jenny outside. She doesn't lock her door, which Jenny finds logical; why lock up a shack?

Already, the sun beats down with fierce, oily heat. They will all melt. Jenny should have insisted on a hat for Benjamin, but she won't risk further delay.

Getting Hattie and Benjamin settled in the car takes forever. There is Hattie's pocketbook to be situated, and the seat to be adjusted for her surprising height. Jenny must push the entire bench seat back for Hattie's benefit, while she herself can hardly reach the pedals. She considers asking Hattie to sit in the back but is afraid of inciting the old woman's wrath. Benjamin must be made secure on Hattie's lap. Then Jenny discovers with pleasure that he is big enough to occupy the middle of the front seat.

"Make sure you hold onto him, if I have to stop suddenly," Jenny instructs Hattie.

Hattie belches softly, and the odor of coffee fills the car.

Swiftly, furiously, Jenny reaches a decision. She will make this woman talk to her. She climbs into the driver's seat and flicks the levers and dials that control the air conditioning, knowing Hattie couldn't possibly have ridden in a car as nice as this one, with its leather seats and luxurious polished dashboard. Hattie's own two feet are her transportation to the churches that she cleans, a colored church a mile from her house and a white church two miles away. Jenny has seen Hattie afoot more than once on her routes, a creature from another century with calico dress and shabby shoes. Jenny has offered her rides and has been refused, as if she has offered something indecent.

Now that they're in the car, Jenny takes time for herself, a pause of her own, to get back at the old woman. She takes a cigarette from her purse and punches in the car's lighter to make it heat up. After a moment, exaggerating the motions for Benjamin's benefit, gratified by his attention, she holds the lighter to the tip of her Winston, making it glow, then replaces the lighter in the dash. She takes a drag from the cigarette, then another. The air conditioning kicks on, cool and dry, whooshing onto their knees. Benjamin stretches out his hands to the vents.

"Please roll your window down. I can't breathe with that smoke," says Hattie.

"Put your own window down," Jenny dares to say. Anger makes her brave. After a moment, Hattie does. Jenny pulls out of the Johnsons' yard into the road, and they're off.

In moments, they pass one of the churches where Hattie cleans. Let her see how fast it can be reached in this gliding car, as opposed to walking. In the dry heat of June, yards and fields look parched. A few backyard vegetable gardens are visible from the road, with an occasional scarecrow standing guard amid rows of vines and small plants. The bigger, better houses have shade trees. There's an old mansion that is said to have been a tavern back in colonial times. Across the road, there's Shirley Lloyd, Jenny's rescuer, playing with her sisters in high grass. The little girls, out of school for summertime, seem to be chasing butterflies. They'll probably get covered with chigger bites.

She feels superior to these people, all of them, she with her city raising. In this heat, in Washington, Jenny and her mother would plan a shopping trip to air conditioned stores, and have lunch at a fashionable restaurant. But Jenny was married. Is married. Her outings with her mother belong to a former chapter in her life. She should be having lunch with her husband, but her life with the Topiary is no longer real to her. As soon as she saw Benjamin, she forgot all about her husband. Maybe he's looking for her, instead. He might show up at her parents' townhouse like a cat returning from a long adventure, preening himself in his green sweater, without explaining his absence.

Scurrying through the high grass, Shirley Lloyd looks up and waves, and Jenny waves back. It's good to show Hattie that she knows people here. Let Hattie wonder how she has met the local people and made connections so fast.

Cicadas and katydids hum in the trees along the narrow, winding road. Insects strike the windshield and leave powder and smears. Hattie sits silently, looking straight ahead.

"Where's Woodrow today?" Jenny asks.

"Out riding. Working," comes the answer.

"How do you have enough to live on?" Jenny asks.

"It's plenty," Hattie says.

"Do you own your house?"

A long pause, then Hattie says, "It's Benjamin house. Lois, she owned it. When she died, it went to him."

"What about Lois's own mother and father?" Jenny asks. "Are they alive?"

"My son was Lois daddy. He dead, his wife too. I raise Lois from when she little."

"That's interesting," says Jenny. Secretly, she is glad about these revelations: there are few living relatives to lay claim to Benjamin. "So you and Woodrow are Benjamin's legal guardians."

"The only ones," says Hattie.

Clell's face rises to Jenny's mind. The Johnsons are too proud to ask anything of him. "I know how Lois died," Jenny says. "Who were the men who were fighting over her? Did they go to jail?"

"You asking too many questions," Hattie says.

Well, she knew that was coming. Jenny finishes

her cigarette, tosses it out her window, and lights another one. "I'm sorry Lois is dead. I could find out more information from other people. You don't have to tell me anything."

"You ain't sorry," Hattie says. "And who you be asking? Him at the old hotel? He won't tell you nothing."

"I am not going to discuss my friends with you," says Jenny. She switches tactics. "When was the last time you went to Richmond?" Years ago, she suspects.

"Day before yesterday," Hattie says, "to the fish market."

"Did you ride on Woodrow's bike? Him steering and you on the handlebars?"

"A friend drove me," says Hattie. "A friend from church."

"I thought you didn't go to church. I've been over at your house lots of Sunday mornings, and you're at home."

"We go," Hattie says. "You don't know all that we do."

The old woman is a liar, maybe crazy. Jenny lets this pass. Fish market and church, indeed. Yet maybe Hattie does know of a fish market, and Jenny can drive her there, and then, while the old woman's back is turned, Jenny can spirit Benjamin away. Jenny makes her voice very earnest as she says, "Some fresh trout or flounder would taste mighty good. I'd like some for my supper tonight. Will you show me where the fish market is, after the doctor appointment?"

"Today's Thursday. It's closed," Hattie says. "They out catching the fish on Thursdays."

Oh, baloney, Jenny wants to say.

They're nearing the city limits, and traffic is heavier. She turns onto broad, leafy Monument Avenue, and the sudden beauty of the street distracts her for a moment, as if her former life, in which she dreamed of romance, is reaching out and tapping her on the shoulder. She is older and wiser now. She knows what she wants in life—and it's this little boy sitting right beside her, staring up at the tall equestrian statues of Confederate heroes, all majesty and verdigris in the summer heat.

"You may ask me some questions, Hattie," Jenny offers. "You haven't asked me anything."

"Nothing I want to know," says Hattie.

Downtown, the streets grow steeper, and Jenny has to concentrate on keeping her place in traffic. She weaves through the intersection of Sixth and Grace Streets. Somehow, the street signs look tiny and hard to read.

"Watch out!" Hattie says, and Jenny brakes hard so as not to hit a pedestrian that she hadn't noticed.

Throngs cross at the corner, men and women in business suits and hats, shoppers with bags bearing the names of stores: Montaldo's, Berry Burke. Haze makes a scrim in front of Jenny's eyes. Bakery smells and café smells float through the air conditioning vents. Benjamin inhales sharply. There's the scent of diesel fuel, too. A city bus cuts in front of Jenny.

The bus turns, and Jenny reads a banner on its side: *Mad Man Dapper Dan*. What kind of product is the slogan advertising? Hair pomade, she guesses, or cars. Her mind works rapidly, even as she searches for the address of the doctor's office, turning, heeding one-way signs. Everything looks a little blurry.

"What street you looking for?" Hattie asks, and Jenny, fuming, tells her.

Hattie says, "We on it."

"Then find the office that says Eye, Ear, Nose and Throat," Jenny commands, angry that Hattie seems to know Richmond better than she does, or is pretending to be able to see better.

"It right there," Hattie says.

Jenny parallel parks, embarrassed that she bumps the curb. She is now fully enraged at Hattie, this arrogant old woman who always seems to get her way, who has possession of the most wonderful person in the world.

Jenny bursts out, "What is it you *want*, Hattie?"

Hattie stares straight ahead. "I don't want nothing, leastways nothing from you," she says. "I got all I ever wanted."

Jenny gets out of the car and slams the door. Hattie doesn't offer to help with change for the parking meter. Jenny fishes coins from her wallet while Hattie and Benjamin ease out of the Lincoln, with much maneuvering on Hattie's part of limbs and pocketbook and little boy. Benjamin reaches up to touch the parking meter, a blazing smile on his face. Jenny swoops down and lifts him up in her arms. His bare knees are still cool from the car's air conditioning. With an expression of wonder, he regards the teeming streets and sidewalks.

Right next to the doctor's office is a photographer's studio. Wouldn't that be lovely, to have a picture of herself with Benjamin? Do they have time?

"It'll only take a minute," Jenny says, pushing open the glass door, which bears the stenciled words, *Photography by Murad*. Hattie follows.

The man at the counter might be a swami. His dark face reminds her of Clell's.

"I want my picture taken," Jenny says, "with this little boy."

"Right this way," the man says and leads her to a corner of the studio.

An elaborately carved chair is positioned in front of a tapestry backdrop. Jenny takes a seat, with Benjamin on her lap, and the man clicks on lights so bright that Benjamin blinks. Jenny shades his eyes, to help him adjust to the light, then lifts her hand away. She is aware of Hattie glowering at her, close by.

Hattie says, "I want to be in the picture too. I'm his great-grandma."

The man looks at Jenny, as if asking if this is acceptable.

Jenny makes them all wait for her decision. She fusses over Benjamin, saying into his ear, "Here's my cute little boy."

The man says, "Are you comfortable?" What kind of accent does he have? Jenny can't place it. A mustache-and-turban voice of silks and spices. She looks at his feet, expecting turned-up, pointed shoes such as Aladdin might wear, but finds sneakers and socks instead.

"I want to be in the picture," Hattie insists. "I b'long in it."

Jenny smells incense and some sort of strange food. Sandalwood and curry, she bets. Do they burn the curry and eat the sandalwood? She can't remember. A beaded curtain separates the studio from some chamber beyond it. The man must eat and sleep in those back rooms, perhaps with a woman and children of his same breed.

Hattie steps into the brilliant circle of light, hovering beside Jenny's chair. Jenny wants to forbid this, but she relents.

"Oh, all right," she says. "And then," she directs the man, "take another picture of just me and Benjamin. Take a whole bunch to make sure you get some good ones."

The man fiddles with a camera mounted on a tripod, peering through lenses and twirling dials. Then he turns around and opens a wooden chest. He fumbles around in it as if searching for something. Jenny sits absolutely still, hoping Benjamin won't get restless.

"Ah, here she is," the man announces, holding up a puppet, a marionette, Jenny realizes. "Cinderella."

He sets the thing on the floor, a heap of strings,

wires, and sticks, and sets about untangling it. He slips a hand through loops at the top of a rope. He lifts the pile of cloth and wood from the floor, and the doll jerks to life, a tiny beautiful woman in a frayed dress, her painted face winsome and startling. Benjamin reaches for her. Quickly, the man is at the camera, manipulating the marionette with one hand.

Just like that, the shutter clicks, and a sharp flash makes Jenny blink.

"Good," says the man. He brings Cinderella nearer to Benjamin, and the little boy beams, holding out his hands. Cuddling him, Jenny can't resist touching the fat part of his cheek. Cinderella swoons. The photographer brings her close and then dances her away. Her dark hair looks real, glistening and wild, like a gypsy's. She is Cinderella before the glass slipper, Cinderella in her days of ashes, poverty, and evil stepmother, yet her face is alight.

Benjamin makes a sound, a gurgle, then a cry: "Ahh!"

The camera clicks again.

Did she imagine it: that Benjamin spoke?

"Madame," the photographer says, gesturing to Hattie, and she steps aside. Jenny is relieved. She expected resistance. But the man recognizes that Jenny is in charge, and Jenny knows that Hattie does, too. The realization fills her with satisfaction.

Cinderella pirouettes and dips, tossing her hair, skimming just above the floor. The shutter clicks over and over.

Only then does Jenny's mind truly register the fact that Benjamin actually made a sound. For the first time, she has heard his voice, an "Ahh!" that is his own. Thrilled, she hugs him, laying her cheek on top of his warm head. Cinderella ventures closer, and with a clacking of wooden limbs, drapes herself on Benjamin's knees, while he strokes her face. The strings connecting her to the man's hand are no more visible than cobwebs, and the shutter clicks again and again. Jenny has never felt so alive, despite another headache starting up, a worm of pain in her head.

Then the man snaps off the brilliant lights, and Jenny closes her eyes, sinking back into the chair. Benjamin relaxes on her lap. When Jenny opens her eyes, the man is hanging the puppet on a hook on the wall. Cinderella is a doll again, trapped in her fable. The contraption of wires and slats knocks faintly against the plaster and then grows still.

Jenny is crying. Her tears surprise her, this sudden waterfall on her cheeks, these drops sliding onto Benjamin's head, onto the soft fabric of his cotton shirt. She hugs Benjamin and rocks him to and fro, her chest shaking. The photographer offers her a box of Kleenex, and she plucks several, but she is too overcome to use them. The man leans forward with a white handkerchief, the kind doves might fly out of, and wipes her cheeks with it.

"That doctor office be closed time we get there," comes Hattie's voice.

Jenny sits up, still clasping Benjamin.

The man says, "I will have the pictures ready for you in an hour. One hour." He holds up a gold pocket watch as if she might not understand.

"Where did she come from?" Jenny asks, nodding toward Cinderella.

The man smiles. "She was part of a traveling show," he says, "far away. She belonged to some entertainers who were passing through Istanbul. My grandfather fell in love with her. He was a photographer too. This camera was his, back then."

Fell in love with her. Doesn't Jenny know how that feels? Didn't she see Benjamin, and have to have him? And now she has heard his voice, his exclamation, "Ahh!"

"He stole her," the man continues. "He had to have her. He took her one night after a show, and then the entertainers were after him, so he stowed away on a ship and came to America."

Hattie steps forward and yanks Benjamin from Jenny's lap. Jenny stands up, but her legs are shaky.

"All right," she says, as much to herself as to the others. "Let's go."

§

The ear specialist declares that Benjamin will never hear. "Profoundly deaf," he says, and goes on to talk about special devices that have benefited a few individuals, "a few highly motivated people," he adds. "Going from a silent world to a world of sounds isn't as easy as you might think. In any case, that's a choice this little boy will probably never have."

Jenny has braced herself for this. She filled out all the paperwork that the receptionist handed to her, waited patiently with Hattie until Benjamin's name was called, and then had to insist, quite firmly, on being admitted to the examining room with them. Once there, she was glad that the doctor addressed his remarks largely to her, no doubt divining that she is his equal in intelligence, more capable than Hattie of understanding medical science. The doctor's own ears sprout tufts of gray hair, like an animal's, and Jenny wonders if this helps him to hear better. She will not give up. The tufted ears are not going to get away without helping Benjamin.

The headache that started at the photographer's studio is bad now. She will ask the doctor for aspirin. But first, she has to concentrate.

"Could something have been done for him sooner?" she asks.

"No," the doctor says.

"Isn't there anything...?"

"Sign language," the doctor says, "as soon as possible. My nurse can give you that information. You will all have to learn it, to communicate with him," and he includes Hattie in this remark. "There are schools for deaf children. Enroll him when he's old enough."

"He understands *me*," Jenny says. "I know he

does. He looks at my face, and I know he can hear me or at least read my lips."

The doctor says, "He can live a fairly normal life. Many deaf mutes do. People will think he's slow. And he may be. His development is certainly delayed because of this impairment."

"Deaf mute? But he spoke," Jenny says. "Just today, a little while ago. We were having pictures taken, and Benjamin talked."

"Made a sound," Hattie corrects. "Went *ahhh*."

The doctor nods. "That may happen occasionally. Don't ever expect him to speak normally, if at all. People can't, when they don't hear language. His language will be sign."

"But," protests Jenny and feels she has hit a wall. This is too much to bear, when she has hoped for hope itself. Can it be enough that Benjamin will hold all her secrets, unable to hear or speak but able to see right into her heart? He looks so tiny on the examining table, calm and intelligent, sitting there. Then he lifts his head and looks into Jenny's eyes.

Suddenly the air is humming. Everything in the room is vibrating: the metal instruments, the light fixture, and Jenny's very teeth. It's the purling of a brassy bell, and at first, she doesn't recognize it. She believes it has something to do with deafness, or with disappointment, that this is what happens when a prognosis is poor. She shakes her head, trying to clear her thoughts, but her brain is a gong.

"Fire alarm," the doctor shouts. He makes a

sweeping motion with his hands toward the door. Out in the hallway, an uproar ensues, as staff and patients rush toward the exits.

The doctor says, "Everybody out," but he doesn't wait for Jenny, Hattie, and Benjamin to go. He ducks out of the room.

Now, Jenny's instincts tell her, and she reaches for Benjamin, wrapping her arms around his shoulders. But Hattie's quick arms are around him, too.

"Give him to me!" Jenny cries.

There is a crushing pain in her foot. Hattie is stepping on it. Jenny kicks, but Hattie moves aside, so she's kicking empty air. Jenny won't let go of Benjamin, and neither will Hattie. They are locked in a tug-of-war. Beneath Jenny's hands, Benjamin is rigid. Jenny thrusts Hattie away and holds onto Benjamin, but the old woman grabs a handful of Jenny's hair and pulls it. How can anybody so old be so strong?

"Let go of me!" Jenny commands, but Hattie pulls harder. "Help me, somebody!" Jenny yells, but nobody helps her. She lands a slap on Hattie's face, then a good hard punch on Hattie's arm. Hattie releases Jenny's hair but wrenches Benjamin away. Jenny screams his name as he slides out of her hold. She knots her fingers into his shirt, but Hattie is right there in her face, reeking of sweat and starch and rage, clawing at Jenny's hands, her voice a hiss that rises above the fire alarm: "He ain't yours, never will be."

Jenny shoves the heel of her hand into Hattie's

nose, feeling the old woman's teeth against her palm. She is dimly aware of Benjamin backing into a corner. She seizes Hattie's shoulders and hurls her backward. Hattie knocks into the examining table, and the table slides into a shelf of glass containers, which tumble to the floor and break. Hattie lunges toward Jenny, roaring. Wildly, Jenny searches for some defense. The doctor left his clipboard on a chair. She picks it up and holds it over her head, crouching. Hattie's boxer-like jabs keep coming, her fists striking Jenny over and over. At last, Jenny stands up and pushes the clipboard into Hattie's middle. The old woman snorts, stumbling.

Benjamin leaps between them, clinging to Hattie, raising a hand toward Jenny to block further blows. Jenny freezes, holding the clipboard in midair. Slowly, she brings it down and lays it aside. Hattie's chest heaves and her lips move, but all Jenny can hear is the alarm, ringing on and on. Hattie's furious eyes hold Jenny's gaze.

Finally, Hattie straightens her dress and takes Benjamin's hand, and together they go out the door into the hallway, where others are hurrying toward the exits. Jenny stays behind, panting.

The doctor pokes his head back into the room and yells, "Everybody out."

Jenny reaches toward him for help, but he's gone again. She springs into the hallway, falling in with the crowd. She has got to catch up with Hattie and Benjamin and get Benjamin, once and for all, yet the noise of the alarm and the staggering, shouting throngs of people make her feel confused. Who would have guessed there were so many people here? But it's not only an ear office; it's also for eyes, noses, and throats.

Already, she feels bruises forming on her body. There is blood on her arms, and her blouse is torn. She should have taken the time to wash at the sink in the examining room.

"Hattie?" she calls. "Hattie, Benjamin, wait for me," but she doesn't see them. They can't be far ahead of her. Strangers' heads and shoulders block her view. The alarm fills her head, ringing down her spine. A man stands in front of the elevators, gesturing people away from them with motions like a safety patrol's, and the crowd veers toward a stairway. Maybe there really is a fire in the building, and this is not just a drill. She always loved fire drills in school, the respite from routine, yet there was always such disappointment when you had to go back inside. Jenny's feet clump along with all the others. The metal stairs shake with the motion of all these people. She calls again, but there is no sign of Hattie or Benjamin.

Suddenly, she's outside in blinding light, the crowd eddying away on the sidewalk. There is her car. The meter has expired. She bumps into a man in front of her.

"Sorry," she says, and as he turns around, she recognizes the ear hair of the doctor who just examined Benjamin. "I didn't have time to pay," she tells him.

"We'll bill you, Mrs. Havener," he says. "You put your name and address on the forms, didn't you?"

"Yes, I think so," she says, scanning the crowd for Hattie and Benjamin.

"What happened to you?" the doctor asks, pointing to her ripped blouse.

"Nothing," she says, too embarrassed to tell him the truth.

The doctor regards her with a keen, searching expression and says, "Somebody attacked you."

"It was kind of, well, a misunderstanding. Benjamin is supposed to be with me, not with her," she says. "Were you finished with us?" she asks. "I was hoping for better news. Isn't there anything that can be done for Benjamin? If I don't help him, nobody will."

The doctor shakes his head. "It's very unfortunate about that little boy," he said. "Does his grandmother work for you?"

"She's his great-grandmother, and I'm a friend of the family." Jenny's voice trails off as a flash of bright green, like a Christmas tree, crosses her line of vision. Bright green, like the Topiary's sweater. "I thought I saw my husband," she says to the doctor.

"Did he come to the appointment with you?" the doctor asks.

"He left me a few months ago," Jenny says. "He always wore this bright green sweater, and I just saw a green sweater. It probably wasn't him, though."

The doctor says, "I'm asking you one more time

what happened in there, after I left the examining room. What kind of misunderstanding are you talking about, with that woman?"

If the doctor's tone weren't so combative, she might answer him, but his stance and his fixed, beady eyes make her feel threatened. There is probably some law against fighting in a doctor's office.

"Don't try to tell me you fell down the stairs," he says.

She holds her hands over the scratches on her arms while she insists, "Nothing happened. A lot of people pushed past me, is all."

"You and that woman had a fight, didn't you?"

"All that got broken was some glass jars," she says desperately. Is he going to make her go back inside and sweep up the shards? She won't do that, because then he might lock her in the room and have her arrested.

She and the doctor face each other for a long moment. He is so close that she believes his ear fur is picking up her very heartbeat. At last, with a frown and a shake of his head, he edges away as easily as a sliding door might retract into a wall. She still didn't have a chance to ask him for aspirin, and now her head hurts so bad, it's as if somebody aimed a slingshot and struck her in the skull. The street noise is so loud, she can't tell if the fire alarm is still going off inside the building or not; no fire trucks have ever come; but that doesn't matter. What she needs to do is locate Hattie and Benjamin, and then maybe this day can be rescued after all, if they stop at the Clover Room for sundaes or milkshakes. Both, if Benjamin wants both. She'll be good from now on; she won't try to take him again.

Unless, of course, an irresistible opportunity presents itself. Once they reach the Clover Room, she can send Hattie to get more spoons or napkins, while Jenny and Benjamin dip into their sundaes. Then, Benjamin in her arms, and a dash for the door — but first, she has to find them.

The heat makes her squint. The street is so dusty, as if there's been no rain for a hundred years. She goes to the parking meter and plunks another dime into the slot. The dial burns her fingers as she turns it.

Where on earth are Benjamin and Hattie? Why didn't they come straight back to the car? A bus, sleek and silver, rolls to a stop beside her. *Mad Man Dapper Dan*, reads its big side. People push past her to climb aboard. She steps back, tired and very hot. Yet why isn't she sweating? She touches her armpits and finds the cloth of her blouse dry. Her mother would be horrified by Jenny's checking her armpits in public. She touches her forehead, but her face isn't sweating, either. Her tongue feels thick and spiny, like a cactus.

Suddenly, there are Hattie and Benjamin right in front of her, Hattie with the familiar fixed glare, Benjamin beaming, reaching toward her, seated on the lap of a woman whose beseeching face looks familiar.

"Oh!" Jenny says, recognizing herself. She's staring into the window of the photography studio. Evidently, the photographer has had time to develop a picture, enlarge it, and place it among these others, photos of brides, babies, and graduates. In the glossy picture, Hattie's eyes glow like a grizzly bear's, dark and ferocious. And to look at Benjamin, you would never know there was anything the matter with him.

Jenny steps away from the window and stands on tiptoe to look up and down the street, through the crowd. She no longer hears the fire alarm, but the street is noisy enough on its own. Still no sign of Hattie and Benjamin. Where could they be? Why aren't they looking for her as hard as she is looking for them?

Well, they can't get very far without her. Is it the bright sun that is making her so dizzy? She'll pay for the photographs and try to find something cool to drink. Maybe the pain in her head is being caused by heat.

She pushes open the door of the studio, and as before, the man looks up from the counter and nods. He says, "Many people have stopped to look at the picture of the young lady and the Negro baby and grandmother."

The remark would please her except that she feels so odd. The room seems dark after the brightness outside.

"How much?" Jenny asks. He gives a price, and she reaches into her purse for the money.

"Where are they?" the man asks. "The boy and the old lady? Are they waiting for you?"

"I don't know where they are. The fire alarm went off at the doctor's office, and everybody had to get out."

"You love that little deaf boy a lot. You wish he belonged to you."

"How did you know he was deaf?" Jenny asks.

"I was looking at you," the man says. "The way your face looked when he made a sound."

Suddenly, Jenny's legs give way, and she leans over the counter. Swiftly, the man comes around it and pulls up a folding chair beside her. "Sit here," he says. Jenny slumps, resting her head on her knees. The man disappears. She hears a swish of beaded curtains, and he is back with a paper cup. "Drink this," he says. She smells the faint chlorine of city water.

As she drinks, the man lifts her wrist and takes her pulse. "It's too fast," he says.

She tries to say, "I think I have heat stroke," but all that comes out is a mumble. Long ago, as a child, she had heat stroke, and her mother fed her ginger ale and potato chips and made her lie down all afternoon. She'd been playing tag in the backyard. Playing tag with who? She tries to remember, but it's too hard.

The man says, "Would you like for me to call a doctor?" and she remembers then why she came downtown, remembers that Benjamin is out there somewhere, and that she has to protect him and get him home. Strangely, she's getting cold now. Her teeth chatter with chill.

"You're sick," the man says. "There is a doctor's office next door. I can take you there."

"No, that doctor is a complete idiot," she bursts out. It's too hard to explain that it's just an eye, ear, nose, and throat place, and that the doctor wasn't any help with Benjamin and probably wouldn't help with heat stroke, either. "I'll be all right," she says.

She lurches to her feet, clutching the man's arm for support. He's about Clell's size, taller than her husband — did she ever really have a husband? — and she's surprised by his skin and hair beneath her fingers. So Aladdin is real, breathing, alive.

"I have to go," she says.

"You might pass out," he says. "You are sick, and your arms are bloody."

"Tell me what happened to your grandfather," she says.

The photographer looks at her with concern.

She jerks her chin toward the puppet on the wall. "The man who loved Cinderella," she says. "The one who taught you how to take pictures. Was he happy, once he had her?"

"In all the years I knew my grandfather," he says, "he was not a happy man."

"If people have what they want, then they're happy," she says.

"It was bad enough to take a puppet," the man

says. "It would be very wrong to steal a little boy."

Jenny pushes past him and out the door, onto the blinding sidewalk. How dare he presume to know what she is thinking, even though he was right. Are her plans written all over her face? Nobody is nice anymore. People are horrible, judging and scolding her. She had sat before his camera so trustingly, and he read her mind, and that is ghastly.

No Benjamin and no Hattie, so what can she do but search for them? She is too woozy to drive, so she goes on foot. The pavement scorches her feet through her shoes. Blocks later, she realizes she has forgotten the pictures. She hates the thought of facing the strange man again. Awful of him to take her money and not make sure she had the pictures.

Even if she had ripped Benjamin from Hattie's grasp at that last instant, she would have to live with the fact that he loved Hattie more than he loved her. It was Hattie that he jumped in front of to shield, not Jenny. Even if she and Benjamin were on their way right this minute to a place where they would be safe — San Francisco or New York or Canada, or maybe Mexico — she would have that sad knowledge in her heart.

She stops walking. She doesn't know where she is, with the afternoon shadows making deep canyons of darkness between the buildings, and the sun burning a torch down the middle of the street, where cars crowd and honk. Maybe she should drive on back to Glen Allen. She might pass Hattie and Benjamin on the way, and she could offer them a ride, and Hattie would have to accept, because you can't make a little boy, hardly more than a baby, walk nine whole miles.

She can't call them, because they don't have a phone.

And she can't remember how to get back to her car. No pictures, no car, no Benjamin.

If she keeps walking, sooner or later she'll come back to the street where the studio is located, and where the meter beside her car must have expired again. To think she was supposed to have lunch hours ago, at the Clover Room, with Benjamin. She is weak with thirst. It should be easy to find a restaurant or a drugstore soda fountain, and order something, but she doesn't think she could speak.

She has been lightheaded and disoriented almost since arriving in these places—Glen Allen and Richmond. She sits down on a bench at a bus stop. She could go home to DC. She could get a job as a secretary for something to do, and spend her weekends shopping, and eventually, she'd be bound to meet a man that she could love, and together they would be good to the children they would have.

But all of that would require turning her back on Benjamin.

Where is her purse? She reaches beneath the bus stop bench, searching all around her, but the alligator-skin, envelope-style purse that she'd bought eons ago in Washington, DC is gone, and her five thousand dollars too. Possibly she lost it blocks ago and only just now missed it.

Rush hour comes and goes, and suddenly, it's evening, with a different crowd on the streets: people at leisure, heading to restaurants, movie theaters, playhouses, and even nightclubs, for surely there are clubs nearby, maybe even the nightclub where Benjamin's mother died in crossfire. If Jenny stands up, she'll be swept along by the crowds as she was swept along during the fire alarm, so she stays where she is. She hasn't had anything to eat or drink since early in the morning. Her heart aches even worse than her head. Her scalp is tender from Hattie's attack, and there are painful scratches and hurt places all over her arms, shins, and feet.

Hattie must be sore, too. The thought brings crushing shame. Jenny remembers trying to gore Hattie with the clipboard, and she feels sick at her stomach.

Benjamin's face comes back to her, too, his huge pleading eyes and the way he leaned into Hattie's dress, protecting her.

She lingers on the bench, but buses keep stopping, and it's too much trouble to wave them away, so she gets up and keeps on walking until the streets are almost empty. She believes she has gone round and round in a wide rectangle of city blocks, for some of the buildings look familiar, but in the dark, there are no easy landmarks to navigate by. There is only the pavement beneath her stumbling feet. Her car must have been towed away. She will have to find a cab to get back to Glen Allen. There are still a few cabs on the street, and shadowy passersby whose glimmering faces meet her own when she draws near to them and then sink away as she keeps on her aimless course. This is what her mother always warned her about—don't stay out late alone, always know where you are, always have some money with you, call for help if you're in trouble. Well, her whole life is in disarray, and she has only herself to blame.

If only it weren't so hot and dark. If only she had a cigarette, but her cigarettes are in her purse. It's the first time she's thought of cigarettes in ages. Well, since this morning, when she smoked in the car. She has been so distracted that she could probably quit smoking without even meaning to. Maybe nicotine addiction is causing her headaches. Maybe Clell is right and there is arsenic in the water at BUY SELL TRADE. Maybe she should get the water checked, but how in the world do you find a chemist? The very thought is exhausting, to try and track down a chemist to come out and tell you what's in water, when water is just water, and all the time that she would spend thinking about the water is time she would not be with Benjamin.

The shock of physical combat is still with her. She has never fought with anybody before.

A sudden throb in her temple makes her stop in her tracks, her hand to her head. Maybe these headaches mean she really is sick.

The Topiary, confronted by the ghost he saw in

her parents' townhouse, might have taken the ghost as an omen that Jenny did not have long to live. If this is true, and if she had known she were going to die, would she have done anything differently? No, comes the answer. It's worth it to have come to Virginia and found Benjamin, even if she has lost him.

"Miss," a voice calls. "Miss, I must speak to you."

She turns around. A shape moves out of the thick dusk, a man coming toward her: the photographer. She stops. What on earth could he want?

"I've been trying to find you." He's out of breath. "These belong to you," he says and hands her a paper bag. "Your purse and photos. I put them in here so people wouldn't think I was a thief, walking around with a lady's pocketbook."

Jenny takes the bag. She swallows over the dust in her throat.

The man says, "Your car is where you left it. I put change in the meter all afternoon, so you wouldn't get a ticket."

"I'm lost," Jenny says.

"Come this way," the man says, motioning up the street.

"I can't find Hattie and Benjamin. I don't know where they are. Have you seen them?"

She's walking in step with him. It feels good to be with a person again. He says, "They probably went home."

"I'm sick," says Jenny.

The man takes her hand and tucks it into his arm. "Lean on me," he says.

At last, they approach the Lincoln, the only car parked on the empty street, under a high, foggy light. Jenny strains to see through the dusk. Something in green detaches itself from the fender. Her heart pounds. It must be the Topiary, who has recognized her car and is lounging beside it, waiting for her to return. She will have to be Mrs. Havener after all, yet life will be simple again, with her decisions made for her. The green form hurtles toward Jenny so that she gasps, holding out her hands to ward him off.

Beside her, the foreign man gives a whickering laugh and plucks something out of the gritty breeze: a green trash bag.

"You thought this was something different than what it is, didn't you?" the man says. "You thought it was someone?" He shakes out the bag. It's just a big green sack, limp now.

Jenny says, "I thought it was my husband."

"That means you need glasses," the man says.

The Bell Over the Door

THIS TURKISH PHOTOGRAPHER, WHOSE NAME is Murad, allows Jenny to sleep and rest all night and all the next day in his rooms behind the studio. He brings her pastries from a bakery down the street. His beaded curtains click back and forth as he waits on customers and comes back to check on her. She hands him her car keys, and he moves her car into a little alley behind his studio. She can see it through the window, her parents' Lincoln, waiting for her to climb back in behind the wheel.

She isn't ready. Her head throbs. Her tongue and her very brain still feel parched from her long day in the heat.

"Keep drinking," says Murad, handing her a glass of water with lemon and sugar stirred in. "And when you are ready, go get your eyes checked."

A whole new day passes, then another. She does go to an optician's office, where her eyes are examined and found to be near-sighted, and she is fitted for a pair of glasses. Wearing them, she emerges into a world so sharp and brilliant that she cries, "Oh."

Her headache is gone. She is the one whom Woodrow Johnson should have given his spectacles to, not that annoying child Shirley Lloyd. Thanks to Murad, she can see again. She might have realized that need herself, if she hadn't been so tired and miserable.

This is what heartbreak feels like. She will have to get over Benjamin. There is nothing to do but forget about him, try to put him out of her mind for five minutes at a time and then ten, and then eventually, maybe several hours might go by when she doesn't think of him. Her heart is a furnace, heated to blazing by her fixation, a bursting, fiery furnace which now must cool off degree by degree. She sleeps in her clothes in Murad's bed, in his clean, sparsely furnished room. He sleeps on a sofa in his studio, drawing the blinds over the big window that faces the street, so that little slats of light shine in. She goes out into the studio one night to look at him. He sleeps on his side, with both hands folded beneath his cheek, as if he's flying on a magic carpet. The studio smells of the rice and meat that he cooked for their supper, some kind of lamb or beef, she thinks. The smell is in Jenny's hair, a savory scent.

She goes to the door and turns the handle, then steps out into the street and regards the framed enlargement of the photograph that Murad took of her and Benjamin and Hattie. It's shocking to be outside again in the city air, out in the world after her withdrawal from it. A laughing couple, holding hands, steps around her. A car passes with its radio blaring a song Jenny used to know.

She can see the picture so well, even in the dark, thanks to her new glasses. Hattie looks three-dimensional, bold and proud. Jenny lets out her breath in a sigh. Hattie won. Benjamin will never belong to Jenny. There is just enough light from the street lamp for her to see Benjamin's face, for her heart to break all over again. She lets her head fall into her hands and she cries, and she thinks, This is it, I can't get past this. Her chest burns, and sobs choke her.

The studio door opens, and Murad is there beside her. "Want me to drive you?" he says. "We can go to their house in the morning. Or right now, if you want."

"I can't," she says.

"Let's put the picture away," he says. "It will be better then."

Together, they rearrange the front window. Soon, the film version of Benjamin and Hattie and Jenny is stacked inside a closet, and pictures of anonymous brides, babies, and graduates fill the empty spot. Jenny finds some comfort in arranging pictures of strangers in ways that catch the unreal light of nighttime. Moving around in the tight, stifling confines of the window, Murad smells of something exotic that might be frankincense or myrrh. Jenny's hands perspire on the framed photographs. All the people in these pictures have been in Murad's studio, yet nothing of them is left behind, not in the way Jenny can still sense a trace of Benjamin when she looks at the chair where she held him just a few days ago.

It would have been stupid to kidnap him with that photograph there for all the world to see, as if she'd created her own "Wanted" poster. She had not thought of that at the time. She would have made a terrible criminal.

And now she has lost him, when so recently, she had believed he could belong to her.

She crawls out from the display window, goes to the carved chair, and stares at her hands, her empty arms. Benjamin must be asleep, nine miles away in Glen Allen, nine miles that might as well be a million. Did he and Hattie reach home safely? Were they able to catch one of the buses that serve the country routes? Remorse and alarm flood through her. Anything might have happened to them as they made their way back to Glen Allen on that terrible day, the little boy frightened, the old woman wounded, and both worn out, just as she was.

Jenny can't bear to think of how she beat up that elderly person. She could have killed Hattie. It is possible that she has hurt Hattie enough to cause an early death from internal injuries. Jenny feels sick at her stomach. She ought to be prosecuted. At the very least, she should apologize and try to make amends, but she knows that Hattie never wants to see her again. To seek forgiveness from the Johnsons would be to place another burden on them.

She closes her eyes and bows her head, but she can't think clearly enough to pray, can't recall even the familiar ritual prayers of church services.

She never meant to cause harm to anyone, and look what she has done. She had thought it was love that she felt, and maybe it was, but it was something else, too, a monstrous invasion of a family. It was destructive, yet it was also the deepest love she has ever felt.

It was right here in this chair that Benjamin spoke for that one and only time, saying, "Ahh." Right here, on Jenny's lap. She drops to the floor and hugs the chair, sprawling face down. She takes off her new glasses and wallows, burying her face in the leather cushion. She cries so hard that she vomits, the remnants of her meal of lamb and rice spewing onto the chair before she can turn her head. To never again hold him or smell his skin. She cries and vomits until her throat is raw, and her eyes are so swollen she can barely see. Around her, Murad is mopping the floor and swabbing the chair. She smells disinfectant. Gently he raises her by the elbows and seats her on a hassock. She rests there for a long time.

Murad prepares to open his studio for the day. He must have been doing this all those days while she rested and slept. He is after all a merchant and a tradesman. He unlocks the cash register. He takes a bottle of Windex and paper towels and cleans the display windows outside and inside. Jenny can imagine him saddling camels with the same ease.

From a cupboard, he takes a vase of artificial flowers, a white plastic cake topped with a toy bride and groom, and a tasseled flat hat like the one Jenny wore when she graduated from high school. He places these objects in the display among the photographs, then goes outside to check the effect.

"Well?" asks Jenny. "How does it look?"

"Something is missing," he says. "Too plain."

"The doll," Jenny says. "Put Cinderella in the window."

"Someone might fall in love and steal her again," Murad says. "It is too great a risk."

Will anyone ever fall in love with Jenny enough to want to steal her? If she possessed the mystery of a beautiful doll, the passive energy of a marionette, limp and lovely until jerked awake by strings, she would be more compelling than she is now, an ordinary human woman. She yearns to be loved as Cinderella was loved by Murad's ancestor. It would be wonderful to be loved that much. She has never had that love, not from the Topiary, nor Clell. They received her love, but they did not give it back. She must have scared off her husband and Clell. That doesn't matter, because she didn't really love either one of them. What she gave to them was herself, all right, but it was only affection.

She did love Benjamin, more than any mother

has ever loved a child. In fact, having children of her own would not make up for losing him; she doubts she could love her own as much as she loves him. Did he love her back? *Yes*, her heart insists, though her brain says coolly, maybe, maybe not. What she felt for him was a sort of holy obsession. She will never understand it. It is with her still. It will be with her until she dies, a physical pain that she breathes in, breathes out, with nobody to replace him, no grief so great as this. He opened up something in her heart that she had not known was there, that craving to give love, and the sorrow that followed, all of it sorrow except when she was with him.

She knows now why people throw themselves off bridges and cliffs and buildings, why mothers sometimes take their children with them when they do that. It would be so easy to make her way back to Glen Allen and lie down on the tracks and wait for a train to come. This is how people must feel when they are close to making that decision. You start having the thoughts, and the thoughts suggest methods — guns, pills, nooses, gas, except Jenny isn't sure how to turn off a pilot light in a gas oven, only how to turn one on, and she doesn't know if Murad's stove is gas or electric, and she doesn't want to make a mess that he would have to clean up, since he has been so kind. She could take off her new glasses and run blind into the street, and she need never see the car or truck that would run her over. Or a bus. *Mad Man Dapper Dan* would be the last words she would ever read. There would be fumes and darkness, noise and weight, and then nothing.

Being stuck in that coffin and riding it down the stairs was easy, compared with this.

She goes to Murad's phone, picks up the receiver, and dials the operator. "I'd like to place a collect call," she says.

Within seconds, she's connected with her father. "Jenny-girl!" he says. "How are you? Your mother and I have been so worried."

"I want to get my marriage annulled," Jenny says, "or get a divorce, either one."

"We were just having breakfast," her father says.

She pictures him chewing his cornflakes, a napkin tucked into his shirt.

He suggests, "I could hire a private eye to look for your husband. How about that?"

"No thanks, Dad. I just want the lawyer's phone number," she says, meaning their family attorney. She will handle this herself. She will not ask her father to do anything for her.

Her father gives her the number, and she calls the lawyer's office and asks for an appointment. This wish is granted, and she hangs up the phone. She will have to drive to DC tomorrow, or if that is too much, if driving a hundred miles is beyond her, she can take a bus. She goes to the little bathroom in Murad's hallway, the one that customers use, and washes her face and hands, amazed that the mirror shows her to be unchanged, except for the new glasses, from the Jenny she was just a few days ago. Yet she has changed inside; it is happening even as she leans toward the mirror. Her head is clear, her stomach easy. Throwing up has always made her feel better, that sense of being level again. She remembers the suitcase in her car and fetches it. The clothes are hot and wrinkled, the toiletries sticky in their plastic containers. She brushes her teeth and changes into a dress which feels too big, gapping at the waist.

She returns to the front of the studio and takes her place at the counter.

Murad is with a customer, taking pictures. The bell on the door jingles, and a woman walks in and says to Jenny, "I'd like to pick up my photos."

Jenny starts to say, I don't work here, I'm just a friend. The woman gives her name and waits, expectantly.

Jenny reaches into the box where Murad keeps the pictures that are ready for customers. She flips through until she finds the right packet.

"How much do I owe you?" the woman asks. "Oh, there it is."

The amount is written on the packet. The woman hands Jenny the exact change.

"Do you need a receipt?" Jenny asks, wondering how she will generate one; she could write something on a scrap of paper.

"No," the woman says. "Thank you." She steps out the door.

Jenny sees what could be—working here with

Murad, having slipped into his life, and he into hers, by merest chance. Tomorrow, she will go to DC and meet with the lawyer. She could move back in to her parents' house, her childhood room, or she could get a nice apartment on Kalorama Circle. But what she wants, she decides as she spreads out her fingers on the glass-topped counter, is to learn how to work the cash register. Murad can teach her how to take pictures, too, for she believes she would be good at that; she will be able to read a face, will anticipate the "Ahhh" that a child might say. Her new glasses will allow her to see into the bright spots of an iris of an eye. She envisions shopping with Murad in dim, cluttered shops for marionettes to keep Cinderella company, to delight the children who will come to the studio.

Has she been under a spell? Has she been sick, in body and in mind, too? No illness but love would leave a person feeling this way.

She will go to DC, but she will come back to Richmond. That is a decision that she makes, as the bell on the door jingles again and someone else appears—the postman. He hands her the day's mail as if she has worked here for years, and she takes it, knowing she can learn to help run the studio, learn how to keep the books and pay the bills.

Murad and a customer are laughing as he snaps pictures. This customer wants a photograph of herself to put in the paper along with her engagement announcement. Her mother is with her, and an aunt. All of the women are wearing bronze rouge, pale lipstick, and too much perfume. As soon as they leave, Jenny will prop the door open and air the studio.

Here she is with the day's mail in her hand, and the flash of the camera a bright occasional flare in the corner of her eye, and the counter a sturdy barrier between her and the world that seems suddenly kinder and more accepting now that she is part of commerce, not a strange isolated person wandering the roads around Glen Allen. She sees tomorrow: yes, she will be able to drive to DC, where she will meet with the lawyer and sign some papers. She will hug her parents and visit with them. Time will pass, and her divorce will become final. Everything in this moment assures her that this is true.

The sunlight on the studio floor looks gold. As the women leave — mother, aunt, daughter — Jenny smiles and opens the door for them, and they sweep out onto the sidewalk with a final draft of perfume. Jenny props the door open with a brick.

"You did well," Murad says, coming up beside her. "Would you like to work here?"

"Yes," she says, and with that word, she says yes in her mind to another vision of the future that is brought to her with the sunlight and traffic and street noise: she will let him take pictures of her, all of her, with nothing on except a scrap of satin. He will know how to make her beautiful. He will make her legs look long, make her feel like a splendid dream of herself. She thinks that they could love each other, but it will be a kind of love that she cannot yet imagine.

"Show me how to work the cash register," she says, and he demonstrates, and she learns right way. All morning, she rings up purchases: photos, frames, and reprints. She books appointments over the phone. No one asks her who she is. She does not have to explain herself.

At midday, she tells Murad, "I've got an errand to run."

"All right, take your time," he says, as if this is a routine day, as if they have managed the studio together comfortably for a long time, yet she believes he understands what she has to do.

She ventures into the alley behind the studio and gets in her car, which smells musty from disuse. She has got to go to Glen Allen.

Her hands shake so badly that she can hardly steer. As she maneuvers out of the city, she tries to think what she will do if she learns that Hattie and Benjamin never got home.

In the space of the last five days, the landscape has changed. The meadows are wilder under a hot purple sky, the grass taller in the fields, the old road narrower. Rain splashes down on her windshield, swirling into the grime on the glass. Lightning rakes the sky, and thunder crackles.

BUY SELL TRADE shows only dark windows when she passes. The steps of the old hotel are deserted. Rain falls harder, thick drops that make her think of Murad's beaded curtains, striking the car in a hectic rhythm that matches the thrashing of her heart.

And there it is — the Johnsons' house, with Woodrow and Hattie jerking clothes off the line, their backs to the road, while Benjamin races around the yard, his arms raised to the sky. Wind tears green leaves from trees and sends them spinning. Jenny can hear Hattie's and Woodrow's voices, high and excited. Woodrow lifts the full laundry basket, and Hattie scoops up Benjamin, and they all vanish into the house.

Hiding behind the rain, Jenny does not think they saw her.

From her purse, she takes the thick envelope of money that she had planned to use for travel with Benjamin. With a pencil, she writes on it, "I am sorry. I will leave you alone."

As lightning slashes the sky, she leaps from the car, dashes to their steps, and wedges the envelope beneath the door. There is just enough space that she can slide it all the way into the kitchen, where just behind the door, the Johnsons might be pouring coffee. Sprinting back to the car, she falls on the slick grass, but she gets up so fast that the lightning bolt is just flickering out as she slides behind the wheel.

The rain follows her all the way back to Richmond, its sweet fresh smell a kind of goodbye. It makes puddles along the rural roads, fills the ditches, and floods the downtown streets. Her tires create great wheels of water.

She will never go back to Glen Allen, not if she

lives in Richmond for the rest of her life.

She has never known anybody more selfish than she is. She has tried to buy her way out of wrongdoing. Yet she is so relieved to have seen the Johnsons, to know that they are all right, that she still can't stop shaking. A new, strange sensation blooms in her stomach: hunger.

She parks the car in front of a restaurant, hesitating. Flowers thrive in the restaurant's window boxes, dripping with the fresh rain. The flowers decide her, and she hurries inside. She orders deviled crab, fruit salad, and chocolate silk pie. Days it seems since she has been hungry, since she has consumed a full, hearty meal from a plate.

Afterward, she steps out onto the wet, steaming street. The rain has stopped. A beauty salon is right next door, and she makes her way inside, where a stylist waves her into a chair.

"I'd like a wash and set," Jenny says, "quickly, if possible. I need to get back to work."

"Of course," the hairdresser says, and turns on the faucets in a deep shiny sink.

And suddenly the world is back in place, though Jenny's heart still aches. Suddenly, a new slip claims center stage in her mind, a satin slip that she might buy and wear for those lovely photographs that Murad will take of her. Then the slip and the photographs vanish and she thinks *Benjamin*, as the hairdresser removes Jenny's glasses and guides her head backward into jets of warm water and lathers her scalp, *Benjamin*, and his very name is a knife in her chest. *Benjamin*—and rinse water sprays her head, so pleasant, even as she steels herself against the hurt of loss. *Benjamin*—and back in Glen Allen, years are going by; her clothes dry-rot off their hangers; her bed and her dishes are carried away by scavengers, by bats. *Benjamin*—he will grow up without her, without even the memory of her, though if in fifty years she passes him on the street, she will know him at once, will reach out for him, *oh Benjamin*.

If he grows up. A shudder runs through her. She cannot, really, imagine him at any other age. She will never know if he learns sign language or goes to school, or if he ever leaves the house with the big stump in the yard, or if he ever makes any other sounds. She can only wonder. She doesn't have the right to find out.

The stylist wraps Jenny's hair in a towel so tightly that Jenny's eyes are pulled back; without her glasses, all she can see of her face in the mirror is an egg, yet the egg is sort of pretty. *Benjamin* — and there comes the new slip again, the slip like a banner in her mind, a shine of future happiness.

Her hair is clean, but her body still wears the sweat and old cells of days without washing. Tonight she will bathe for a long time. These last hours in her worn clothes, her old skin, are almost a thing to savor.

The stylist shakes out Jenny's hair. Newly long, it covers her eyes, her whole face. The hairdresser parts it with a comb that glides sharp as a needle down Jenny's scalp, and lifts it away like a curtain. Only then does Jenny reach for her glasses, so that she might find the clear outlines, the details, the subtleties, that have been there all along.

The author wishes to thank the National Endowment for the Arts and the University of Memphis for support provided during the writing of this story.

About the Author

Photo by John Bensko

Cary Holladay grew up in Virginia and Pennsylvania. She holds degrees from the College of William and Mary and from Pennsylvania State University. She is the author of four previous books: *The Quick-Change Artist: Stories; Mercury; The Palace of Wasted Footsteps;* and *The People Down South*. She is the recipient of a National Endowment for the Arts Fellowship, the Goodheart Prize, and the O. Henry Prize, among others. Her husband is the writer John Bensko. They live in Memphis, Tennessee.